like a
HURRICANE

like a HURRICANE

like a HURRICANE

RAVENPEAK BAY
RIA WILDE

Copyright © 2023 Ria Wilde
All rights reserved

The characters and events portrayed in this book are fictitious. Any similarity to real persons, living or dead, is coincidental and not intended by the author.

No part of this book may be reproduced, or stored in a retrieval system, or transmitted in any form or by any means, electronic, mechanical, photocopying, recording, or otherwise, without express written permission of the publisher.
ISBN: 9798862799309

Cover Design: Ria Wilde
Formatting: Ria Wilde
Edited by: Amanda Wallace

Author note

Like a hurricane is book 2 in the Ravenpeak Bay series. This book is set on a fictional island with a fictional town inspired by the islands off the coast of Maine.

Each book is an interconnected standalone with crossover characters. It can be read on its own but is best enjoyed when read in order. To read in order, start with These Rough Waters, which follows Torin and Maya.

This book has several dark elements that some people may find triggering. These include violence/murder on page, grief & loss of a parent, light stalking, bribery & blackmail, kidnap & the use of drugs for sedation.

This book follows Torin's brother, Everett and heiress Arryn Lauder. It is sexually explicit throughout and contains scenes which include some light primal play, light dom vibes & period play.

It is recommended for mature readers 18+

Ria

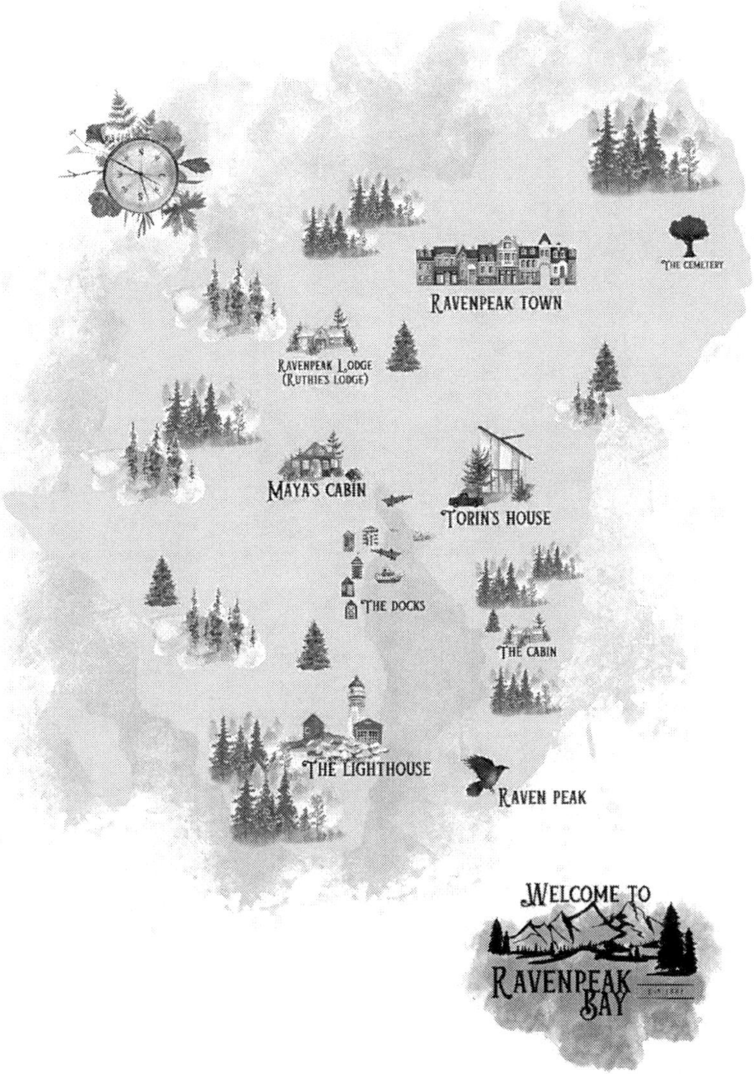
Ravenpeak Town
The Cemetery
Ravenpeak Lodge
(Ruthie's Lodge)
Maya's cabin
Torin's house
The docks
The cabin
The lighthouse
Raven peak
Welcome to
Ravenpeak
Bay

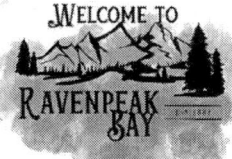

PROLOGUE
everett

My shoes clip against the shined marble floor of the Lauder Hotel in central Portland, Maine. A crystal chandelier hangs from the high vaulted ceiling, casting a golden hue across the burgundy paneled walls that are home to several rare pieces of art, the frames lavish and gilded, reflecting the light. A couple of well-dressed staff man the front desk, greeting everyone with a professional smile and ending every sentence with a kind 'sir' or 'ma'am'.

It was the kind of place I often found myself in. You see, it isn't the criminals and the masterminds hiring my kind of services, it's the businessmen wanting to take out their rivals, it's the wealthy, and prestigious husbands, and wives wishing to take out their

spouses. Either because they've been wronged, humiliated or divorced and are facing destitution.

Death solves a lot of these people's problems. Always has and always will.

This was no different.

Victor Lauder is CEO of a very successful and luxurious set of hotels and resorts across the United States, and he's called on my special set of skills to eliminate a competitor. It isn't a case of being better in business and the likes, not when he has the kind of money to solve the problem without ever having to lift a finger.

It's my first job back after I was injured and put in a coma two months ago. I figured why not start again with a simple job, especially when the payout was phenomenal, and the target was going to be easy. And I didn't even have to travel far after spending so long on the island with my brother and his new wife.

"Good morning," I greet the young receptionist, her blonde hair pulled back in a tight ponytail, white shirt stretching over her ample chest. Color rises into her cheeks and her eyes widen as I give her a smile and a slow perusal of my eyes, "I'm here to see Victor Lauder. He's expecting me."

"I – he – please hold," The woman stammers, more color blooming on her pale cheeks.

It was early January, and the weather was as predictable as ever, it either snowed or it was overcast with the threat of snow looming. You'd never believe I am a sun man, not when I spend so much time in places that rarely see the sun, but fuck how I'd love to be

laid out on a sandy beach right now.

"Mr. Lauder, sir," the woman stutters into the phone, bringing my attention away from the obnoxiously large doors and the white blanket covering the city, "There's a gentleman here to see you."

"Who?" She repeats, panicked eyes jumping to mine.

"Everett Avery." I tell her.

She repeats my name and then nods furiously, as if the man on the other end could see her. "Of course, sir," She rushes out, "I'll send him through right away."

She struggles to get the phone in the cradle, clearly flustered, "Mr. Lauder is ready for you now, Mr. Avery, if you'd just go through those doors there," She points to the labeled 'Staff Only' doors, "He's the first door on the right."

"Thank you…" I pause, glancing at her gleaming gold name plate, "Penny, I'll be sure to tell him how helpful you've been."

She blushes and I stifle my eye roll at how easy it is, weighing up how much I need a good fuck, since it had been a while, or if I just wanted to get this over and done with. I could have sweet, blushing Penny on her back before the clock struck half past ten if I wanted.

Hey, three months is a long time. I was stuck on an island with my brother and his new pretty wife for months after I was in a coma. A man has needs.

I don't knock on Victor Lauder's door once I've made it through. He's a balding man, age lining his face with deep wrinkles that pull on his eyes and mouth. He's tall and looks relatively fit otherwise and as I let myself into his office, ignoring the gleaming gold name plate attached to the door, his eyes swing to me.

"Mr. Avery!" He jumps up from his large red oak desk, black suit pressed to an inch of its life, and hurries over to me, hand outstretched in greeting.

"Mr. Lauder," I dip my chin, accepting his hand.

"Please take a seat," He gestures to the shiny leather chair in front of his desk and as I take it, he settles back behind his desk, straightening his tie, "I appreciate the haste in which you responded to my email."

I dip my chin again, falling into that persona everyone who has heard of me knows. Sure, outside of the job I had fun but when I was working... I wasn't the same man.

"I assume you looked over the file I sent you."

"I did, Mr. Lauder. You wish to take out your competitor and his only son, Kenneth and Malakai Ware."

He swallows, "Yes."

"Well, you came to the right person," I confirm, reaching out my hand for the file, "I require a fifty percent advance before the job is done and the remaining once I've sent proof the job is complete."

"Five hundred thousand, right?" Victor pulls on his

collar, "For the whole job."

"Correct," I flip open the file, flicking through the small square photographs attached by paperclips to the front page, a selection of images of the father, the owner of an up-and-coming range of new hotels and resorts and his only son, and heir to his enterprise.

His hope was to end them both and put a stop to their growth and remain the front runner for his wealthy clients.

"I can have it completed in a week." I tell him.

"A week!?" He chokes, "Why so long?"

"Because Mr. Lauder, I need to understand their patterns and movements, need to ensure a clean and thorough job or you'll end up exactly where you are now, dwindling profits and clientele."

He huffs, "Fine, but no later. I want that bastard and his son gone. They've taken enough of my business."

"And I'll make that happen." I assure him, pulling the card from my pocket, "Pay the advance into this account, I assume I don't have to tell you to keep it dark."

He nods and picks up the phone, dialing someone who answers on the first ring. It's as he is speaking with whoever it is, that I hear the very feminine clip of heels on tile. The rhythmic sound has my head turning slightly so I can look over my shoulder.

And when she fills the door frame, her long cobalt blue dress clinging to every curve and dip of her body, glossy black hair pulled across one shoulder and a pair of sunglasses covering her eyes, I lose my breath.

Because the woman that just entered, has sucked every ounce of air from my lungs and stolen the oxygen right out of me.

I feel it when her eyes, still hidden behind the glasses despite the weather outside, land on me and her lush plump mouth curls up on one side in a sultry little smirk.

"Dad," She turns her focus to the man behind the desk once he's finished on the phone, "I need to speak with you for a moment."

My phone pings with a familiar sound – money being deposited into my account – and I stand, turning to face the woman head on.

Breathtaking – that's the only way I could describe the woman. Utterly devastating. Like a hurricane wreaking havoc on a poor small town.

"He's all yours," I tell her as I turn my focus back to her father, "I'll be in touch."

CHAPTER ONE
arryn

"A salad for my date," the man across from me orders, folding the menu as if he has any right to choose what I eat.

"I think the fuck not," I hiss, snatching the menu he has refused to let me look at since I sat down at the table. I scan the items, "I'll have the twelve-ounce ribeye," I tell our server, "Medium rare."

I feel the eyes of my *date* glaring into me from across the table. I don't even know why I bother dating sometimes, they always end one bad way or the other. This one just happens to be ending right before it can begin. I'll be the bad guy I always am, and rumors will circulate, like they always do.

"Listen carefully now, James," I address him when

the server has scurried away and not in earshot to listen to me dress down the dumb fuck in front of me, "Do not ever, and I say that literally, *ever*, believe you have the right to order food for a woman. Do not think you have any opinion on what she puts in her mouth or body, and do not believe I will sit here and let you control how this evening goes."

Red blotches his cheeks as his eyes widen, but I don't let him spew whatever sentence is on the tip of his tongue as I continue.

"I am a grown ass fucking woman," I growl at him, "I can eat and drink and do whatever the hell I want to. I am a prize. You… You're nothing more than entertainment for me, I was very bored when I accepted this date and I realize now, I would have been better off with a tub of ice cream and an episode of *Sons of Anarchy*. At least Jax never lets me down."

I sip my white wine and lean back in my seat, watching the mix of emotion wash across his face. First, it's confusion… *How could this happen to me? Me!? I'm rich and drive a Benz, I have a pool house!* Then it's anger… *Fucking bitch, I hope she chokes on an olive.*

And finally, we have – *let me placate the girl so I can still get her on her back, and tell my buddies I railed the ice bitch from the Lauder Hotel.*

"Arryn, sweetheart," He starts, "I just assumed you were a salad girl. I won't make that same mistake next time."

I scoff, "Next time? There isn't going to be a next time. In fact, there isn't even a *this* time. I checked

out of this date five minutes ago, I'm just here for the steak, girls got to eat after all."

"You're a bitch," He sneers, screwing up his napkin and throwing it down onto the table, "Pay for your own food!"

"I was going to," I stare down at my manicured fingers, buffing them to a shine on the breast of my silk dress I'd chosen for this evening, "After all, I do earn more than you."

His face turns a shade of red to match the color of the sports car I crashed last month, "Fuck you!"

"Ta-ta now, Jack."

"My name is James."

"Close enough." I shrug.

He storms from the fancy restaurant, tripping over his own two feet as he goes and I just grin into my wine.

Perhaps I was the problem.

But I know my worth and that man can't afford it.

When the food arrives, and the poor girl realizes I've been ditched, her face loses all color.

"Don't worry about it, babe," I shrug, grabbing the cutlery on the table, ready to dig into my food, "He wasn't worth it, but I am hungry!"

She sags in relief, "What about his dish?"

"I'll pay for it," I tell her, "Go ahead and enjoy it, or

give it to someone who will."

"You're Arryn Lauder, right?" She hovers, chewing on her lip.

"I am."

"You're incredible, Miss Lauder. Really."

I dip my chin, "Thank you." I say and dig into the dripping steak on my plate.

I stack my dishes neatly on the table for the servers to take away, cradling the bowl of my wine glass in my palms as I survey the crowded restaurant in the heart of Portland. It reminded me of the foyer in dad's hotel, all burgundy walls and gold accents. I don't know why that was the color scheme the rich decided showed wealth but here we are. I knew most faces sitting at each table, like the producer two tables down sitting with a woman who isn't his wife, or the woman enjoying a meal with her tycoon husband, even though she's going to divorce him soon, despite the smile on her face that says otherwise.

I grew up in these circles and continue to move in this crowd. I don't have many friends, or family. My dad, Victor Lauder, and my sister, Olivia, are the last remaining blood relatives I have.

As the eldest daughter of a man who owns a luxurious chain of hotels and resorts tending to the richest and most powerful, there are expectations of me. But fuck if I would let a man control me, even if it goes against

what is taught to women like me at a young age.

I decided to step away from the hotel game young and went into modelling. I'd made a name for myself.

The Arryn Lauder.

Model. Entrepreneur.

I'd not only dominated the modeling space, but I'd come out with a line of lingerie to compliment all and every body type. And I'd ensured it was affordable.

After the modeling and business, I was heiress to the Lauder Hotels and Resorts.

I didn't want my father's business but knew it would come to me, nonetheless. My younger sister, Oli, would be a better fit, but she was overseas studying, and my father had made it clear the business would come to me, regardless of whether I wanted it or not.

I was sick of having my choices taken away.

But I'd figure it out. I always did.

Taking the last gulp of my wine, I let my eyes wander around the dining room, hoping to snag the attention of the server so I could get the bill, but my eyes fall on someone else instead.

A man.

He sits at the wall length bar on one of the high-backed leather stools, nursing a whiskey out of a crystal glass, and his eyes are on me.

And I recognize this particular man, I mean how

could I not?

Tall, standing around six foot four, he towered over me back at my father's office only a few days ago, his handsome face is lined lightly with stubble and his glacial eyes feel like they could touch every deep dark part of my soul. He's ridiculously attractive, with his dark hair cropped short at the sides but left longer on top, letting it flop boyishly, charmingly, over his forehead. Dark, thick brows set over expressive blue, grey eyes and framed by lashes that would make any woman jealous.

And he has a dimple.

One that indents his right cheek when he grins.

And good Lord, *that* grin.

He looks like he's stepped right out of a novel and is living up to every book boyfriend fantasy I had ever had.

Because let's be honest, the only good man is a fictional one.

Call me bitter, I don't care.

I'd dated enough men to know they all had their own red flags, each one much worse than the last.

And despite this pretty face and no doubt killer body beneath his expensive suit, the man at the bar may as well have had a neon sign flashing above his head that read stay clear, I'm either a misogynistic ass or I'm a playboy and I'll break your heart.

Neither of which I was in the mood for.

I had a photoshoot in the morning for a perfume ad, followed by another shoot in the afternoon and I needed to get some sleep now that I had been fed.

When the server returns, I pay for the food and drinks and gather up my belongings, tucking my jacket over the dusty pink dress I'd selected for the evening, tying the belt around the waist to keep it tight and step out from the table.

I give polite smiles to everyone who greets me on the way out but as soon as I'm out the doors, I suck in a clean, fresh breath of icy winter air. Snow was falling – what a shocker – adding to the growing blanket already settling on the city.

I keep away from it to save the white Louboutin's on my feet and call my driver from my phone.

I shiver against the chill while I wait.

The door behind me opens and I feel the presence of a body step up to mine. A subtle glance to the left shows the man from the bar has stepped up next to me.

"There's a whole sidewalk for you to wait on," I note.

"Hadn't noticed," His deep timbre of a voice chases away the chill in my spine.

He smells so fucking good, it was unfair, like aged whiskey, spice and musk. It made me want to bury my nose into his neck and inhale.

"Do you mind?" I swallow.

"Not at all, Miss Lauder," He glances down at me, "Are you cold?"

"No." I lie.

He chuckles and shrugs out of his jacket, laying it in a way so only the fabric touches my body and not his hands, "Your ride is coming around the corner. Get home safe, Miss Lauder. Keep the jacket."

And then he walks away, disappearing around the corner of the restaurant in just a shirt that stretches generously over the broad expanse of his shoulders as my driver stops on the snow-covered road ahead of me.

And even though the car was warmed and the seats generating heat, I tuck the jacket closer, holding the lapels together with my hand and do what I wanted to do on the sidewalk. I inhale that intoxicating scent.

CHAPTER TWO
arryn

Six out of the seven days I was working. If it wasn't a shoot, it was an ad, if it wasn't an ad, I was down at the factory approving new lines of lingerie to add to the stock for the online shop. And if it wasn't that, I was at the Lauder Hotel in the middle of Portland, helping my dad, even though he had thousands of members of staff on hand.

I was busy.

And tired.

The sound of my heels on the tiles is as therapeutic as one might find the rain on a tin roof. There was just something about the steady, strong tap of my shoes on the floor. I loved the sound and mostly chose to wear heels.

The love for heels started when I needed those extra inches in height, as a model I was already shorter than average, and at the beginning of my career, I didn't want a single part of my body, especially a part I had no control over, to affect my chances of success.

And the first year of wearing these things on my feet, I loathed it, until one day, I didn't. Granted they aren't the most practical pair of shoes, but it isn't like I'm about to go hiking in them.

My PA chats animatedly at my side, her fingernails tapping on the screen of her cell as she answers my emails. Without Suzy I was damn sure I would have burned out and cried in the corner somewhere a long time ago.

She was a life saver.

"After the shoot this afternoon," She chirps, aiming her sunshine smile in my direction, "You're free. You should be out by three!"

For a Saturday that wasn't bad and the tub of ice cream in my freezer was calling my name.

I could see it now, feel it. I'd change into my shorts and tee set, settle under the thick knitted blanket thrown over the back of my couch and dig into the tub of cookie dough ice cream while the TV runs old episodes of *Friends*.

Such simplicity was the dream.

"Miss Lauder," The current marketing head for the perfume brand I was shooting for today pops his face around the door. I hadn't memorized his name, they

usually quit in the first month, and I only knew that because I've been the face of this brand for the last five years. "They're waiting for you down in hair and make-up."

"Thanks Kevin," I try anyway.

"It's Kurt."

I wince and give him an apologetic smile while mentally patting myself on the back for at least getting the first letter of his name right.

My face is powdered and blotted, hair plucked and primed before they maneuver me down to the dressing room, hands grabbing at the clothes on my body.

"I am quite capable of dressing myself." I shrug out of their grabby fingers, stripping the rest of the way down and grab the – "What the fuck is this?"

The thin gold ropes of material dangle from my fingers.

"Your wardrobe," Harriet, the wardrobe coordinator, stammers nervously.

"I wasn't told I'd be semi-nude for the shoot."

No, I didn't have a problem taking my clothes off for the camera, fuck there were likely sex tapes all over the internet of me, and I didn't really care but warn a girl first!

"The perfume is literally called 'Stripped'." Suzy says breezily, "Should've expected this, Ryn." Suzy was the only one who called me Ryn. Come to think of it,

Suzy was probably the only friend I could rely on, but that was only because I paid her.

Well, isn't that a sad crock of shit.

Grumbling, I take the material and duck behind the screens to take my underwear off and replace it with this gold...*thing*.

It goes in places it definitely does not belong but with some adjustments, ensuring the lady bits and nipples are completely covered – a feat in its own right – I step out and head down to the room for the shoot.

I'm there for three hours, my body contorted into unnatural angles, oils applied to my skin, wind blown in my face while the gold body suit chafes, and my muscles scream in protest at all the poses I have to hold for long periods of time.

I blow out a breath the moment the shoot is called to a close and let myself flop unceremoniously to the floor, staring up at the white tiles and lights above me.

"You good?" Suzy bends over until her face hovers over mine.

"Remind me why I do this?" I groan, rolling my ankles.

"Because you love your job," She lists, "You're a bad bitch who looks *great* behind the camera, and you're fulfilling your childhood dream of being a model."

I huff out a breath.

"Where's the next shoot?" I ask.

"Twenty minutes downtown," She supplies, "We have to leave in ten minutes."

In other words, get your ass in gear, we have to go.

Drowning out the noise, I get up and head back to the dressing room, slipping behind the screens to take off the body suit I hope to never see again. God it was awful, looked great but was awful…

I suppose we could say that about a lot of things in life.

I reach for the underwear I left folded with my clothes and pause.

My bra was there, a cute little lilac number with lace over the cups and a little bow in the bridge that sits between the breasts but my underwear, a matching thong, is missing.

I check under the bench and in the corners. I move all the clothes, separating them out to make sure I hadn't done that thing we all do at the gyno, and tuck them out of sight like underwear was something to be ashamed of but no, they aren't here.

And unless underwear can grow legs and walk out on its own, someone had stolen my panties.

Motherfucker.

I pull the bra on and then my dress, feeling a little vulnerable since I was bare underneath and poke my head around the screen, "Suzy, do I happen to have a spare pair of panties in my bag?"

Her brows tug and knot in confusion, "Excuse me?"

"Check my bag," I tell her.

Stammering, she rifles through my purse but comes up empty with a shrug.

Damn it.

"Someone stole my thong."

She gasps, "I'll call security immediately!"

I roll my eyes, "Don't bother. Not the first time, won't be the last. Think we could swing a stop at a store to grab a pair?"

"We've got seventeen minutes before we have to be there and the drive takes at least twenty without traffic," Suzy grimaces.

"Fuck, okay."

Commando it is. I gather the rest of my belongings and follow behind Suzy, making our way back out into the bitter January wind before I climb into the waiting car.

I was counting down the hours for the day to be over.

I kick my shoes off at the door, landing on the flats of my feet with a sigh and head straight through to my bedroom, turning left to disappear into the walk-in closet, already pulling on the zipper of my dress.

It falls to the floor in a swish of material, and I unhook my bra, standing there naked for just a minute before I head through to the bathroom, shower off the day and then get into that comfortable pair of shorts and tee I've been looking forward to since this morning.

As promised, I was done with the day by three, home by four and on the couch, ordering take out by five. My long dark hair is pulled up into a messy bun atop my head, my skin gloriously free of any product.

I was starting to wonder if it was time to reduce my hours. I did love my job but the more I did it, the less I liked it.

Now the designing of underwear and the overseeing of manufacturing, that was different. I never watched the minutes during that, if anything I wished the clock would slow so I had longer to dedicate my time to it but the modelling, it was becoming a chore.

I had wanted to be a model ever since I was little, watching these gorgeous women splashed across magazines and on TV, seeing them with their make-up done, their hair perfectly styled and clothing looking like it was made for them. I reached that dream and now it was rapidly going downhill.

Not my career, that was as steady and firm as a rock, but my feelings on it.

I flick endlessly through the programs listed on the TV, not picking one until there is a rap of knuckles on my door, my stomach rumbling obnoxiously loud.

A kid greets me on the other side, handing me a brown bag that smelled delicious and scurries away.

But my feet freeze on the threshold, a chill rushing down my spine.

Have you ever had the sense you're being watched? Like you can't see it to confirm it, but you just *know*?

I glance left and right on the street, the streetlights illuminating the packed white snow on the sidewalks, but all is quiet. The snow falls gently, adding to the already thick layer on the ground and a breeze teases the bare branches of the trees that line my road. But there isn't a single person out here, no tracks in the snow other than the ones left by the delivery guy and me.

I live on a very quiet street in Portland, my little bungalow tucked back from the road and there aren't many who know where I live. I've had to deal with one too many stalkers to be careless, and I paid a shit ton of money to keep my property secure.

Yet, I still feel like there is a set of eyes on me.

CHAPTER THREE
everett

They were right there.

Sitting on top of a perfectly folded set of clothes. Light purple, like the color of wisteria and lacy, so soft under the rough tips of my fingers that I couldn't help but tuck them into the pocket of my jacket.

And then I watched her shoot, her tight delectable body wrapped in gold like a present under the Christmas tree. Arryn Lauder was earth shatteringly stunning.

Dressed. Undressed. Sassy or sweet.

A ruin waiting to happen.

Now I wasn't usually one to take notice of my client's

family unless it called for it, but Arryn was an exception. There was no way I wasn't taking notice.

She was like the first storm of the season after endless days of scorching heat. She was the rain and the lightning, the thunder that rattles your windows and the wind that strips your trees.

Just like a damn hurricane, sweeping in to wreak complete chaos.

There was no way to ignore her, no way to pretend she didn't exist. My attention had been so thoroughly snagged I worried I would never be able to focus on another thing.

I followed her to her next shoot, watching her as she posed and smiled for the camera in a pretty blue dress that made her olive complexion pop. Her eyes are an alluring shade of grey, a match to the stormy skies that often plagued the small town I'd just come from, and the only place I could really call home. Even if I hadn't been a permanent resident there for some time.

I'd spent time there these past few months, first visiting my brother who I'd thought was wallowing in grief but wasn't at all, and then I was recovering after being shot. I had a cabin on that small island, one I loved and had built from the ground up, but it was covered in dust and smelled like age and neglect now.

It was home though. Even if I avoided it.

But now Arryn was calling to something deep inside of me, and her panties were burning a hole through my jacket. I stand in a pocket of darkness, the snow coming down gently, like feathers floating in a breeze as it settles onto the already snow packed earth.

She comes to the door to accept the food she had ordered, pausing in the doorway to look left and right down the street, eyes scanning right over me where I remain hidden in the shadows.

She had stolen my attention more than any job ever had, more than any promise of cash. It was the first time it had happened to me, and I never thought I'd find something more tempting than that of a kill.

I didn't know the woman, other than what I'd dug up on her from the web, although that would change after the program I designed and created finished doing its work on pulling every ounce of data on the girl. By the time it was finished I'd have everything on her, down to her favorite color and childhood pet name.

Was it legal? Not even a little bit but the program comes in handy. I just needed a few details about the person for it to work and I could pull text messages and call logs, access medical records, see their GPS tracker from the past three years and access every account ever created under their name, from socials to government accounts. So, no, it wasn't legal, but it was fun. And it always helped that it gave me an edge to a job not many in my line of profession had access to.

The door to her little bungalow clicks closed after some time of her watching for movement and then I see her curtains shift, being pulled tighter to stop any peeping into her house. But she didn't realize that if I wanted in, I would get in. Closed curtains and locked doors were hardly a barrier for me.

And getting behind Arryn's doors was something I wanted desperately to do.

I bunker down, sheltering from the snow while I wait for all the lights to go off some time later and then wait just a little bit longer until I'm sure she is asleep. Following women wasn't usually my go to, I didn't have to most of the time, but there was something about this one that required a little more attention. A more thorough approach, like those storm hunters who chase a tornado rather than run away from it, just to understand it better. Risk and reward and all that.

I open the app connected to my program on my cell, seeing the list of files already collected on Arryn and head straight for the folder labeled 'Security'. Her pin is right there on top and access to the security feed. I first disable the cameras but not the alarm since it would alert her and pick the lock, slipping into the warm house silently. The security panel beeps quietly, and I quickly input the code, disabling it which plummets the house into complete silence, so much so that I can hear the clock ticking on the wall in the kitchen.

Not even my feet make a sound as I move through the place, running my fingers over the furnishings, noting the candles on the shelves and the fresh flowers in a vase on the counter. It smells like cinnamon and spice in here, like she had just finished burning a candle and the scent was lingering in the air.

There's an empty pot of ice cream on the side and a wine glass with a drop of red wine left in the bottom alongside the empty containers of takeout food. The blanket was slightly skewed on the couch, the remotes for the TV left on the cushions.

Coming out of the living space, I head down the hall. Every door was closed except the very last one at the end, and there was a very soft light spilling out between the gap. Moving so I can stay in the shadows and out of view, I head towards that light and peer through the small gap.

The bed is the first thing I see, thanks to the light plugged into the wall – a nightlight I realize – her shape is clearly visible beneath the heavy blankets, her raven black hair spilling out across the pale pink pillows behind her head which is buried into the sheets.

She doesn't stir as I continue to watch her through the small opening but deem it not enough and push the door a little, testing the hinges for any squeaks. When none occur, I push a little harder, opening it up completely and step into her bedroom.

I already had a plan for her father and the job he wanted me to do, this right here, with his daughter was something I had never found myself doing.

It was bad business tangling up with a client's family, but I just simply did not care.

I step up to the side of the bed, opting for the position that gave me her back rather than front. It was best in case she woke up, even if I wanted to see how pretty she looked when she slept. Do her lashes flutter? Are her lips parted as she breathes evenly and dreams soundly?

How does that stunningly devastating face look now that it's rested, and not scowling in every direction, like she had a personal vendetta against the world?

Unraveling this woman was a need like an itch under the skin. A craving dug so deep the only way to sate the need was to fill it. And she was the drug to light up my veins.

I gently lift a section of her hair, feeling the silky black strands catch on the roughness of the callouses on my fingers, becoming a little bit obsessed with how her soft feels against my rough.

Her hair was beautiful, a color so dark it could rival the night sky and long, straight and glossy that I wanted to wrap around my fist and pull, stretching out her long, elegant neck ready for my teeth.

God damn there wasn't another woman like Arryn.

Bending slightly, I lift the hair I have in my fingers to my nose, inhaling the smell of her coconut shampoo.

And then I spend an ungodly amount of time watching her sleep, tucking myself out of sight so she can't see me if she wakes, and I observe each roll and twitch of her body. She tosses and shifts several times, moving to her back and her stomach, her eyes remaining closed and yet she appears restless. Her breathing turns from even to rapid, breaths coming out fast and hard and then she just stops…

And she sits up, a hand clutched to her throat while her stormy eyes scan the room.

Smart girl…

My grin tugs up a little at the edge knowing she won't

see me despite her nightlight.

She looks for a long time, searching for that one thing that feels *wrong*. And when she can't find it, she checks her phone left to charge on her nightstand and then settles back into her bed.

It's only when I can see she is clearly back asleep that I slip out the door, pulling it back to the position I found it in and set the alarm, booting up the cameras again once I'm clear of the house.

I may be able to get through her security, but I'll be fucking damned if I leave it open for anyone else.

Arryn doesn't know it yet, but she is now *mine*.

CHAPTER FOUR
arryn

"Sundays are sacred, dad!" I hiss into the phone while I try to find the other shoe to the nude stiletto I have in my hand, the dress hugging my body pulling taut until I hear a stitch pop, since I was contorting myself into some odd positions to try and rifle through the closet looking for the damn shoe.

I could wear a different pair, but the nude heels were my favorite and the most comfortable pair I own. And if I have to be presentable on a Sunday, I am going to wear my favorite pair of shoes damn it.

"I know, honey," He placates, "I wouldn't ask if I didn't require you in attendance."

"Why exactly do I need to be there?" I shove a couple of boxes out the way, spotting the toe of the missing shoe. "Got it!" I exclaim.

My father huffs, "They're investors," He says, "They've asked for you to attend since you'll be taking over one day, likely sooner rather than later since I'm not getting any younger."

"Dad," I sigh, the shoe dangling from my fingers, "You have loads of time."

But my dad just chuckles, "When will you be here?"

"Give me an hour, I'll be there."

"Thank you, Arryn," He sighs, "I knew I could count on you to show up."

"Yeah," I whisper, "See you soon."

The line cuts off when I hit the big red button on the screen and sag against the wall. I didn't even have time to check over the notice that my cameras went down last night before my dad called to request my attendance.

I'd woken to the oddest sensation of being watched, it had roused me like a warning siren blaring inside my head. But my security was top notch, and yet a niggling thought has me shoving off the wall and moving in the direction of the security panel. I open the log, swiping through the backlog until I see it, and my heart drops into my stomach.

Right there, on the touch screen pad attached to the wall shows my security system unlocking by pin. Only me, my dad and Suzy had the code for my security panel. Even with the stalkers I'd had before, none of them had been able to get close to me.

Pulling out my cell, I dial the company in charge of my security and get through to a woman who sounds bored and a little tired, if the groaning yawn is anything to go by.

"Yes, this is Arryn Lauder," I say before reeling off my security information, allowing her to access my account, "Can you advise if there were any malfunctions last night? Between the hours of eleven PM and two AM?"

"I can see the system was deactivated at twelve fifteen," The woman says impatiently, "and reset at three."

"I know this," I snap, "I didn't deactivate it."

"Please hold."

"Are you serious right –" I'm cut off by static infused hold music. "Fuck."

With the phone pressed to my ear, I head through to my room, throwing myself down onto the stool in front of my vanity so I can at least look fully presentable for dads meeting. Hitting the loudspeaker button, I lay my cell on the table and begin to apply my makeup, my nerves shot while that damn hold music threatens to make my ears bleed.

I'm halfway through applying my liner when the woman crackles back through the speaker, "Miss Lauder?"

"I'm here."

"It appears there was a technical glitch that effected a

select number of customers last night."

"A technical glitch?" I repeat, the knots in my stomach unraveling slightly.

"Yes, ma'am, we are sorry for the inconvenience, but we can assure you our technicians fixed the problem as soon as they were alerted." Her robotic voice grates on my patience.

"And you didn't think it necessary to let me know? I thought someone accessed my home."

"We apologize for the inconvenience."

"Right. Okay." I say, forcing a breath out my lungs and telling myself to calm the fuck down. It wasn't this woman's fault, even if her service left much to be desired. The main thing here was that no one had broken in last night. Perhaps it was just paranoia that woke me and a dream that made me think I was being watched. It happens. I sleep like shit most of the time, have done so since I was kid – *thank you, trauma* – so it wouldn't be impossible. "Thanks for your help."

"Of course, ma'am," She says, "And thank you for choosing Garrison & Son security. Have a great day."

There is no time to even say goodbye since the woman hangs up before I can even get my mouth open.

It was fine, I tell myself. No one was in here.

I finish getting ready and shove my feet into my shoes, plucking up the keys to my car before I exit and lock up.

I have perfected the art of walking in stilettos in all kinds of weather, rain, ice, snow but the damn cold would kill me one day. It has been snowing for the last twenty-four hours and while the roads had been kept mostly clear, the same couldn't be said about the sidewalks. I blast the heat the moment I get the engine on and hit the button to start my favorite playlist before I pull away. The hotel was only twenty minutes from me, so I make it there with plenty of time to spare. Parking in my designated spot under the hotel, I take the elevator to the lobby, sighing with the warmth that chases away the winter chill.

"Miss Lauder," Diana, one of my father's oldest employees smiles kindly at me and I lift a hand in greeting, only to freeze in my tracks.

The man from my father's office and the sidewalk outside the restaurant, is standing in the lobby. He leans casually against one of the marble pillars that stand proudly from floor to high ceiling, legs crossed at the ankles, hands buried in his pockets. Oozing casual indifference and tempting mystery.

I didn't know who he was or what business he had with my dad but there was something *off* about him.

He was as devastating as he was that first day I saw him, all dark and enigmatic like. His mouth kicks up into a half smile when he sees me staring and he dips his chin as if in greeting, his eyes wandering down the length of me in a slow, deliberate perusal before coming back up.

I swallow.

What was it about him that screamed red flags? The boyish, playboy charm he seems to let off? Or was it the underlying threat I knew he possessed? There was just something about him that I didn't quite like.

And I certainly didn't like how he just kept popping up. Had my dad hired me a bodyguard without telling me? That was the only explanation I could think of.

The man starts towards me, and I spin on my shiny nude heel to get away from him. His chuckle sends the hair rising on my arm, "Miss Lauder." He greets, matching my quick pace towards the conference room.

"Who are you?" I ask, "And why do you seem to show up out of nowhere?"

"Everett Avery," His hand on my wrist jerks me to a stop, "Pleased to meet you."

"Well Everett, you're fired."

His brow notches up in amusement, "From what exactly?"

"Whatever my father has hired you for."

"Are you sure you have that authority?"

"Well since whatever it is has something to do with me, then it appears I do." I snap.

At that, he just grins, "Not everything is about you, princess, but I'll be sure to let your father know your opinion on the matter."

"Wait," I grab his sleeve before he can walk away

from me, "You've not been hired as a bodyguard or something?"

His glacial eyes drop to where my manicured fingernails are buried into the material of his pristine suit jacket, "I've been hired by your father but not for you."

"Oh."

"Disappointed?" His eyes flare.

"No." I snatch my hand back, "It's just that you keep popping up."

"Hardly a cause for concern," He cocks his head.

"What about at the restaurant?" I throw back, "Outside on the sidewalk?"

"That's a very popular joint to eat, Miss Lauder, I happened to recognize you after meeting you in your father's office earlier."

"And today?"

"I have a meeting with your father."

"Now?" I check the watch on my wrist.

"It'll only take five minutes."

I still didn't trust him. Not even a little bit.

He smelled good though, something inherently masculine. My eyes drop to his hands, noting the rough texture of the callouses on his fingers and how large they were.

"What is it exactly that you do, Mr. Avery?" I flick my eyes back up to his to see him already staring at me, a heat entering the swirling depths of his eyes.

He wasn't the first man to look at me like that, but I wasn't ashamed to admit he was the first for me to respond to.

There was something very primal in the way he was looking at me right now, something very dangerous and for whatever reason, I liked it.

He leans in dangerously close, so close I feel the breath from his lips brush against the shell of my ear, "Well if I told you that, little storm, I would have to kill you."

I suck in a gasp of air, but he just straightens, winks playfully and strolls away, whistling as he goes.

I'm so shocked that it takes me a moment to realize the tune he is whistling is the same as the last song I listened to on my playlist.

CHAPTER FIVE
everett

I'm still whistling when I step into Arryn's fathers' office and click the door closed. His eyes snap up to mine, "Mr. Avery," He stands.

"Tomorrow night," I tell him, "Your job will be complete by tomorrow."

He swallows nervously, "That's um, that's perfect, thank you."

"I expect the money to be wired within five minutes of you receiving the proof the job is done."

"Proof?"

"You don't want to ensure I follow through with it?"

"Well, I didn't think I would have to see it."

"If you're willing to trust my word, then don't look." I shrug nonchalantly.

"Well if that's all," His voice shakes, giving away his nerves, "I have a meeting to attend."

"Having second thoughts, Mr. Lauder?" I ask.

"Not at all," He straightens his shoulders, "The bastards have to go."

I nod with a grin, feeling the familiar twitch of anticipation curl my fingers. This was a relatively easy job, in and out, quick and clean, not as fun as some of my other jobs but a good starting point after what went down only a few months ago. It had been two months since I killed anyone, the last one was quick and simple too, some bitch not worth remembering after she fucked with my family.

But after this job, I'd find something a little more complicated and a lot more thrilling.

Leaving Victor's office, I step back into the hall to find Arryn waiting there.

"How about dinner?" I say to her, coming to a stop in front of the alluring woman, "Tonight. Seven PM."

"That seems more like a demand than a request," She replies.

"The choice is entirely up to you. I'll have a car stop by at seven. You can either get in it or not. The choice is yours."

"Well, I guess you'll have to wait and see, won't you,

Mr. Avery."

"I guess I will." I grin knowing damn well she was getting in that car. Her curiosity was far too demanding for her not to.

It helped that I saw her checking me out and knew she found me just as appealing as I found her.

I feel her grey eyes on me as I make my way out of the prestigious hotel and through the large doors into the snow that just won't give up. My feet crunch over the thickly padded snow as I head down the sidewalk and pull out my phone, dialing my brother.

"You need bailing out already?" Torin's deep voice grunts through the phone.

"And here I thought you might miss me," I sigh dramatically.

"What is it, Rett?" He asks.

"Is that Uncle Rett!?" I hear little Harper in the background, the daughter of my brother's wife, Maya, and his new stepdaughter, thus making her my new niece. The kid was adorable, even if her choice of pets was questionable. I mean who chooses a chicken as a pet? Last I checked Ruthie, the owner of the only lodge on the small island I called home, had given the girl the chicken and Torin had made her a small coop in the backyard.

"Let me speak to Harper, Torin," I demand, "She's the only one who appreciates me."

"You're so dramatic, asshole," Torin grunts but he

passes the phone over.

"When are you coming back, Uncle Rett!?" Harper demands.

I thought I hated the island that was home to Ravenpeak Bay, the small little town that Torin, me and our adoptive brother, Kolten had found some years back now. Torin had fallen in love within a few months of moving there and got married, had a son but then tragedy struck, and it seemed to fracture us all. When Torin lost his first wife something changed for us all. Kolten had been acting strange already but that was nothing new for him, he was always a bit of an outcast, as much as I love the broody fucker and Torin became a shell of a man. Well at least until he met Maya, the woman who had completely turned his world upside down.

But after spending time there after so long of being away, I realized I didn't hate it at all. Sometimes it was nice to go into the quiet, to go back to the little cabin I had buried in the woods even if I wasn't sure I could ever leave this life behind. I was raised to kill, it wasn't as easy as just switching it off, no matter how much Torin claimed otherwise.

I'd have to go back soon, I think.

"Soon," I tell Harper, "I'll come to visit soon."

"You better!" Harper orders sassily.

After a ten-minute conversation with the kid followed by a quick talk with my brother, I hang up, taking the steps up to the apartment I owned in the city center. It was kept clean and maintained by housekeepers when

I travel, which I do a lot. The job takes me all over and this week was the first time I'd been back here in months.

It was sterile, a place to sleep more than anything else but I'd stocked the fridge with food and beer and used the place as a base for this contract. I head through to the office that was set up with monitors and PCs running twenty-four-seven, monitoring all the feeds for my targets plus the one monitor I had dedicated to Arryn.

I'd had to make a quick call to her security company and pull a favor with the owner since she'd clocked her security system being disabled last night. Granted, I hadn't expected her to check and that was on me.

If I hadn't been watching the monitors at the time and seen the call, I would never have been able to tap the line and hear it. The owner pulled the strings I needed and settled her but if I was to do that again, I'd have to use a more tactile way of gaining entry to her house.

Though the next time I'm inside those walls, I was aiming to be invited.

Rolling my shoulders, I hit play on the playlist she was listening to in her car and settle back in the chair.

Such a damn easy mission. These circles were all the same, money and business talk, pomp and show. The targets were as average as they come, a father and son duo coming in hot and heavy on Victor's territory or so he thinks. They were just businessmen, smart businessmen with a lot of money and sway in the industry.

Did I think it was worth killing them over? No. Was I still going to do it? Of course, I was. I didn't much care whether the men I was killing had done anything to deserve it. That wasn't my job to do. I took contracts, fired the gun, and took the money at the end of it. Perhaps this one would land me on a beach in Bora Bora. Perhaps I'd even take Arryn with me.

My targets had no special routines, work, bar and gym, day in, day out. They sat in their stuffy offices, in their pressed suits talking numbers over and over. I'd looked into both the father and son, neither had anything worth mentioning which had surprised me some.

Most of these people have *something* to hide but these guys were squeaky clean.

I link my fingers behind my head and glance at the clock. Seven hours to go.

I stand in front of the restaurant, hands in my pockets as the car pulls up out front. The driver climbs out, stoic and professional as he walks around and opens the back door. I take a few strides to the door and offer a hand to help her out of the back of the car.

Her manicured fingers slide over my palm in a gentle caress before they curl around it, and she pulls herself out of the car. The touch of her is like electricity, like the static in the air right before lightning strikes and then my eyes land on her.

She's in a floor length champagne colored dress, the neckline low and the material clinging to her shape, from her trim waist, over the curve of her hips and then down her long legs. Black hair pulled over one shoulder and lips painted a blood red, she has more than just my head turning.

"Arryn," I address her by her first name, watching her lashes flutter as I rasp her name, "You look beautiful."

"Thank you."

I link her arm with mine as I walk in through the doors to the restaurant, smirking at the eyes that follow us through. Her fingers flex where they rest on my forearm.

"You came, after all," I say as I pull out her chair, letting my fingers skim her back as she takes her seat.

"Call it an apology for how I acted before," She dips her chin while I take my seat across from her, calling for the server to pour the wine.

She thanks them and plucks up her glass.

"No apology needed," I tell her, taking in every line of her face, from the slope of her nose to the plump lips and sharp jaw.

"So will you tell me what business you have with my father?"

"Not tonight."

"Well how can you be sure there will be another opportunity?" She swirls her wine in her glass, looking at me from beneath her lashes.

I chuckle. The woman is tough as fucking nails. Another thing I hadn't been expecting. I hadn't guessed it when I met her in her father's office, but I soon realized it after watching her over the last few days. She handled herself with grace while her words were as sharp as the knives I had stashed back at the apartment.

I could see now how Torin became so damn obsessed with Maya without even really knowing her. It was like a magnet you can't ignore.

"Because Miss Lauder, I intend on making you so damn obsessed with me, you won't want to leave my side."

"It'll be a cold day in hell when I become obsessed with any man, Everett, sorry to disappoint."

"Bad history?"

"Not particularly," She picks up the menu, "I've just found men in general to be entirely lacking and rather disappointing."

"Well, they weren't me," I tell her confidently, "I can assure you, there are very few things I lack."

"An ego isn't one of them, I see," She licks across her teeth and quirks a brow but the little pull on her mouth betrays her real feelings on the matter.

"And here I thought confidence was sexy," I wink,

mimicking her by picking up the menu myself.

She laughs quietly while she peruses the menu and I pretend to do the same while I watch her instead.

It was hard to place exactly what it was that had captured me. Was it the raven black hair or the contrast of her grey eyes? Was it the fiery temper? The snappy attitude? Was it that she appeared to be a woman of grace and yet could roast a man to within an inch of his life and then sit back and warm herself by the flames left behind, all while she checks her nails and smiles sweeter than the cookies Ruthie bakes at the lodge?

All I knew was that this woman was born to be mine. Made to be mine.

I didn't care what means I had to go to, to make it happen, Arryn Lauder was going to be irrevocably *mine*.

Even if she didn't know it yet.

When the server arrives, she places her order while side eying me as if I had any say in the matter and then I place my own order.

"So, Everett," Arryn links her fingers beneath her chin, resting her head in the cradle of them, "You won't tell me what you do or what business you have, what will you tell me?"

"I think you're the most stunning woman I have ever seen."

She rolls her eyes, "That's all?"

"What more do you need?"

"Everett," She starts, a sag to her shoulders that wasn't there before.

"Rett," I say, "You can call me Rett."

She quirks a brow as her mouth turns down at the edges, "*Everett,* do you know how many men have said the exact same thing you just said? That have seen me and my looks and instantly wanted me as a prize because they think I'll be a pretty trophy on their arm?"

There it is.

"I don't care if you think I am attractive." She continues. "Quite frankly, it is the least of my concern."

"You mistake me," I lean back, swirling my wine in the glass, "Granted you are stunning, there is no denying that. But I wasn't just talking about your looks."

"Is that so?"

"I'm a thorough man, Arryn, I look into everyone I meet. And I looked into you."

"That's a little stalkerish, Everett."

"You're smart. Driven. Feisty," I grin, "I didn't need to look into that last point, you show that off all on your own and I fucking *like* that."

Her mouth opens as if to speak but I push on, stopping her so she can hear me.

"You own a room, not because you look good, but because you're a presence. You ever got that feeling, when a storm is just about to hit, and everything goes quiet? The air stops moving, the birds and the insects, they stop calling and the clouds roll, bringing in that storm quietly and stealthily, the silence acting like a warning of what is to come."

Her grey eyes flare, watching me intently while her hand stills mid-air, the wine glass held in her long fingers.

"The feeling starts right in your chest, and it travels out, through all your limbs and muscles, it tells you to *look,* to witness it. That's what you do, Arryn, like a damn hurricane, you own all and everything around you and all you have to do is step into a room."

Her lip's part on a small gasp and I lean forward, trailing a finger up one of her own, "You capture me, Miss Lauder." I say, "Completely."

CHAPTER SIX
arryn

I'm not even ashamed.

I step into Rett the moment we exit the restaurant, pressing all of me against all of him and capture his mouth with mine. He tastes like whiskey and bad decisions, and I'd never tasted anything more delicious.

It had been a long time since a man had managed to do anything for me. They were all the same, wanting the same thing, to tie up, to press down, to control but with Everett it felt like I could be myself. I could be unapologetically Arryn with no expectations and no limitations.

He meets my kiss with his own, overpowering it as his hands come around to press into my back, holding me with no escape, not that I was trying. His tongue seeks access between my lips, tangling with mine in a battle of passion and domination. And I was a mess of mixed feelings, part of me wanted to submit, give myself over, and the other part wanted him begging.

So, it was a fight.

Right there on the sidewalk, mouths fused in a kiss so intense it fried my brain of all coherent thoughts until this was the only thing that mattered.

Neither one of us gives up control or power, my hands curling tight into the lapels of his jacket while his palms press firmly on my spine, like we couldn't get close enough. The sound of tires sloshing through melted snow sounds to the left of us but even with an audience, we didn't stop.

"Spend the night with me," He rasps, nipping my kiss swollen bottom lip.

"Get in the fucking car, Everett," I practically growl, attacking his mouth as I push him towards the car waiting to take me home. I only release his mouth to let him climb into the back, the door held open by the driver who looks at everything and anything other than us as we practically fuck each other's mouths with our tongues.

"Rett," He corrects.

"Everett," His name comes out on a moan as I straddle his lap, the dress stretching to within an inch of its life as my legs part to make the distance of his thighs. Then I press down onto his lap, feeling the hard, thick length of him currently tenting the front of his pants. He groans as I grind against it, throwing my head back as my hands grip his shoulders for support and his come down onto my thighs, fingers sinking into my flesh.

"Fuck, Arryn," He groans, guiding my hips in a slow, torturous grind against his cock.

We were like a couple of horny teenagers on prom night, getting off in the back of the limo on the way home.

The journey back to my place flies by in a blur of teeth and tongue and temptation. I was ready to fucking burst and the man had yet to touch me. I was so fucking hot and wet and needy; I was fully prepared to strip him down right now, but then the car comes to a stop and the driver very loudly clears his throat.

"Get out the car, Arryn, so I can take this fucking dress off you and lick every inch of your body."

"Don't tease me, Everett."

"We'll see who's teasing when I have you spread on your kitchen table with your legs over my shoulders."

I just about manage to stifle my groan and get out of the car, my legs like jelly as I feel his body follow mine, sliding up behind me as the door slams and the car drives away, leaving us completely alone on the street outside my house. He presses against the back of me, his chest to my spine, his hand curling around my hip as he tugs me back slightly, pressing his hard cock to my ass.

"What are you waiting for?" He whispers, brushing hair away from my neck so he can press a tender kiss to the space where my neck meets my shoulder.

"Don't disappoint me, Everett."

"Get your pretty ass inside, little storm, let me show you how much I'm not going to disappoint you."

There was a tremor in my hands that wasn't there before.

I didn't get nervous, I didn't get shy or unsure but right now, with Everett, I felt out of my element. And I couldn't figure out why.

"Where should I have you first, princess?" He whispers, guiding me forward. The warmth of the house chases away any chill from standing on the sidewalk, so these goose bumps were all his doing. "Right here in the entrance?" He muses, "Bent over that pretty white couch?"

"Everett," I whisper.

"Louder."

"What?"

"Say my name louder," He demands, "I'll be making you scream it soon enough."

My breath rushes from me as my heart kicks up a notch.

He stops us in the space between my living room and kitchen. Since my place had an open plan layout there were no walls between where my kitchen and living room started.

"We didn't have dessert," Everett says lightly.

"No."

"I'm a dessert man, Arryn."

His fingers grasp the zip at the back of my dress.

"Tell me to stop."

I don't.

The zip slides across the teeth quickly, splitting my dress down the back and I feel the rough tip of his finger graze down my spine before he brings both hands to the shoulders of my dress, and eases them off. The moment the straps are clear of my shoulders, the dress falls away and pools at my feet, leaving me in a set of my own designer lace underwear.

Everett hisses though his teeth.

"Look how fucking stunning you are." He praises.

He guides me to the kitchen, all the while I remain silent, stumped to what I should say and do. What the fuck was wrong with me?

"Sit your pretty ass on the table, princess. Now."

I spin on him, "You think you're in control here?" I ask.

He smirks, eyes bouncing down my body as if to say, *'you're the one almost naked right now.'*.

"You realize I wore matching underwear for a reason, right?" I hop up onto the table, squaring my shoulders and willing some of my power back. "Everett, honey, I have you right where I want you."

He chuckles lightly, "Is that so?"

I reach around to the strap at my back and flick apart the hooks on my bra, letting it come apart and remove it from my body. Everett's eyes immediately drop to my exposed flesh. And even though I feel slightly more in control, my chest still heaves with my breaths, my heart pounding just a little too hard and fast.

He groans, fists curling at his sides as if he is restraining himself from touching.

"Tell me again," I whisper, "Who is in control right now?"

"What do you want?"

I grin. "Touch me, Everett."

The muscles in his cheeks pop as he bites down onto his teeth and grinds. Glacial eyes latch onto mine as he lifts a hand and runs it up the center of my abdomen, trailing the tip of his finger up my sternum and between my breasts, to the dip between my clavicles and then he opens his hand up and wraps it around my throat.

"We can pretend you're in control, little storm," He whispers, leaning in close as his fingers flex around my neck, "If that's what you want."

He presses in harder, forcing me to yield under the pressure of his palm. But I have no complaints about it. I allow him to push me back, fingers twitching around my throat, until my spine presses against the top of my table. He slots his body between my legs, his still covered dick pressing against my center.

"Stay very fucking still, princess," He growls against my mouth before he starts to retreat down my body, kissing and nipping across me. His mouth finds my breast, teeth sinking into the soft tissue on the right side before biting my peaked nipple, rolling it between his teeth and eliciting a guttural cry from me.

He flicks his tongue while his teeth sting, causing a riot of sensation that I can't quite make sense of.

My muscles quiver as he works his way down my body, away from the sensitivity of my breasts and down my stomach until he reaches the band of my thong, his fingers hooking almost delicately into the straps.

His eyes flick up to mine and a feline grin curves up his sensual mouth as he pulls them down, tapping my thigh when he wants me to lift my hips so he can slide them completely off.

And then I'm right there, completely naked while he's still fully dressed.

"Tell me again," His eyes meet mine from between my legs, his breath blowing air across my pussy that was shamelessly wet and aching, "How you're the one in control right now, princess?"

CHAPTER SEVEN
everett

I stare up at her from between her legs, spread out on the table like a feast only for me. Her tan skin is flushed with a pretty blush, her chest rising and falling heavily. She was all toned muscle and long legs, delicate curves and dips and goddamn if it didn't make me want to sink my teeth into her.

Her black hair spills down behind her and her hooded grey eyes watch my every move as I turn my head slightly and press a kiss to her inner thigh. Her throat works with a swallow.

She invited me in. Demanded it even.

This was where we were meant to end up.

I kiss slowly up the inside of her thigh until I blow

my breath across the sensitive flesh of her pussy, reveling in the way her head dips back and she expels a harsh breath. I bring my hands up to hold her open, fingers biting into the softness of her thighs and then I lick, from her entrance to her clit, groaning as her taste alights on my tongue.

She cries out again and again as I worship her pussy with my mouth, sucking her clit between my lips, as I let one hand go from her leg and spear a finger inside of her, her wetness drenching my hand as I fuck her with my fingers.

"Everett," She cries.

And there she goes again with the full fucking name. "Rett," I growl, nipping her with my teeth which forces her to arch her spine and bear down her hips, knees shaking.

"Don't stop, please," She begs. "God, you feel so fucking good."

Hey, I'm not ashamed to admit I'm a man who likes a little bit of praise.

I fuck her with my fingers and focus my attention on that little bundle of nerves that makes her roll her pussy against my mouth, riding me for the pleasure and climax.

"Yes, yes," She chants, "I'm going to come." Arryn moans. I curl my fingers inside of her, caressing that sweet spot just inside and flick my tongue on her clit, eyes looking up at her to watch her face twist with the euphoria of her climax, watching as her lips part and her muscles strain and shake as the walls of her cunt contract around my fingers.

I wanted to feel it around my cock.

But I wanted her to come in my mouth more.

She begins to tremble harder, her moaning becoming louder as I thrust my fingers harder into her and suck her sensitive bud. The taste of her was like fucking honey, so damn sweet and perfect. Addictive.

"Everett," She cries as I continue that torturous pace and then she unravels, crying out loudly as she comes all over my mouth and tongue.

I pull a condom from my wallet and shove at my pants while she catches her breath on the table, hooded and fully satisfied eyes latching onto my hands. I free myself and rip off the jacket, unbuttoning my shirt so I have nothing in the way to restrict my view of sliding into this storm of a woman. I roll the condom on, jerking my hard cock once, twice, so damn hard it physically hurts.

"Open your legs, princess," I order, "Spread yourself wide for me."

She anchors her heels on the edge of the table and spreads herself, her pussy wet and ready for me.

I nudge the tip of my cock into her, eyes rolling back at the first feel of her on me, and have to restrain myself from simply thrusting forward and impaling her on my cock.

"Goddamn, little storm," I praise, "So fucking good."

"Fuck," She hisses, "Do it again."

I oblige, slipping in a little further this time, her cunt stretching to fit me. I was enraptured by the way I was sinking into her tight little body, how she flexed and stretched to fit me. How we joined so fucking perfectly, my body nestled into the cradle of her thighs, sinking deep into her as she mewls so prettily spread out before me.

"More," She demands.

"Goddamn," I groan, my restraint snapping and my hips surge forward to thrust into her hard enough, her body jolts up the table. She swings her arms up and behind her, clinging to the edge to hold herself in place as I lose all damn control of myself.

"Fuccckkkk!" I moan, slamming into her again and again, the feel of her sending me somewhat crazy. I hoist her legs up and over my shoulders, leaning forward to rest my palms on the table as my chin dips and I watch as I thrust into her, over and over again.

Sweat drips from my temples, my jaw slackened by pleasure.

I wanted to ruin this fucking woman. Ruin her and claim her and possess her.

"Harder, Everett, fuck me harder. Make it fucking hurt."

Holy shit.

I snatch a hand forward, wrapping it around the delicate column of her throat as I move in close, "Shut the fuck up, Arryn," I growl, "And take my cock how I fucking feed it to you. You want fucking hard," I thrust hard enough for our bodies to slap loudly together, forcing a cry from her mouth, "Let me give you *fucking hard*."

I rip away from her to stand, gripping her thighs as I adjust to give her what she wants. Hard, rough fucking, fingers bruising, hips pounding.

She screams as I maneuver her into a better position, letting go of one leg to press down on her lower abdomen with the flat of my palm as I hit new depths.

"Shit, yes," She cries, "Like that. Don't stop."

"God, fuck," I groan, slamming into her once, twice, feeling that telling tingle down my spine that warned me I was so fucking close.

"Come for me, little storm," I demand, dropping a hand to her clit so I can circle my thumb on her sensitive bundle of nerves, "I want another one from you, give me another one."

"Oh god," She screams, her pussy fluttering around me so I apply more attention to her, working her up as I thrust harder, my own climax about ready to take me out.

She cries out as her pussy clamps around my cock and the sensation of it rips my own orgasm from me. I grunt, hips sputtering, unable to keep up with the unforgiving pace I was applying and then I'm spilling myself as she too, comes all over my cock.

I collapse onto her, holding my weight as I bury my

face into the side of her neck, licking up the salt on her skin as she breathes hard and trembles beneath me.

"Didn't..." she whispers on a breath, "Disappoint after all."

"I don't plan on disappointing you for the rest of the night, princess."

"Are you one of these rare breeds that is never quite satisfied?" She laughs.

"With you, I don't think I'll ever be satisfied."

"Prove it," She whispers.

"Plan on it, little storm, by the time I'm through with you you're not going to be able to fucking walk."

Her nails score the back of my head, her legs clamped tightly around my waist as I thrust up into her, her back sliding over the tiles of the shower wall. Hot water sprays down onto us, plastering my hair to my forehead as water cascades over Arryn's face, makeup smudged across her eyes and mouth.

And then when we're done in there, her cries of pleasure ringing like music inside my head, I take her on the bed, ass in the air as my fingers bruise her hips and I disrespect her body with sure, hard thrusts, slamming into her over and over. Both our bodies were a mess of finger shaped bruises, of teeth marks and scratches. It was carnal and fucking primal and I wanted her mark on me for the rest of my damn life.

The skin across my back was stinging in the most delicious way, my muscles tight and aching from the physical workout that was *fucking* Arryn Lauder.

And she said I was one of those who wasn't quite satisfied, but she must have been talking about herself. Because this woman didn't know when to stop, didn't want to stop and I would keep giving and giving, with my hands, mouth and cock.

I would mark and taste every inch of her.

I squeeze her firm ass in my hands, loving how big I was compared to her, how my hands could cup her waist and wrap around her throat.

Sliding the same hand up her spine I take a fistful of hair and yank her head back, grinning as she cries out in a mixture of shock and pleasure, stretching out that delicate neck of hers.

I keep my thrusts from behind purposely slow and hard, going in deep, the position of our bodies allowing me to hit a spot I couldn't before. She was slick and dripping, soaking me thoroughly, the slap of our bodies a rhythm I wanted on repeat.

She chants my name as her pussy begins to flutter around me and then she's coming again, clamping around my cock.

But this time when I come, I pull out of her, rip the condom off and give my hard, aching cock a few tugs, spurting my climax over the creamy skin on her back. She collapses down on to the bed in a mess of sweat, slickened skin and hair, shoulders heaving as she catches her breath.

I drop next to her, my come still marking her skin.

She turns her pretty face to me, lids hooded with fatigue. It was late, she was tired. Getting up, I cross the room to the ensuite and grab a warm washcloth before I head back and clean her up.

"Stay," she says drowsily as she tucks herself into her pillows and flicks back the sheets on the empty side of her bed. I pull my boxer shorts into place and turn off the main light, sliding in beside her.

And as she lays there, one arm thrown over my chest, sleep claiming her quickly, I wonder if she knows she just signed her life over to me.

When I find something I want, I don't tend to let it go.

CHAPTER EIGHT
arryn

It takes me a moment to remember the body next to mine, in a bed only I have ever slept in alone, was in fact, invited.

Everett lays on his back, chest bare and breathing steadily in his sleep.

Intricate ink has been tattooed into his pecs, a design of sharp curves and edges on one side and the other was etched with the head of a tiger, smoke and shadows surrounding the art. Across the ribs was cursive writing in a language I couldn't read.

Mors vincit omnia.

I trace the letters with the tip of my finger, wishing I knew what it meant.

HURRICANE

The past twelve hours have moved in a blur of motion, from dinner to the sidewalk kiss that ultimately ended with us both naked and moaning. I'd feared Everett would be like the rest, selfish, controlling and not worth a minute of my time, but I'd been wrong.

That man knew exactly what he was doing, and he did it with such precision, there wasn't a single part of my body that had not been caressed by him. He used and owned me so thoroughly I couldn't tell where I ended, and he began. He certainly did not disappoint.

He was arrogant and mischievous, a playful smirk constantly pulling on his mouth. I would have placed him in the same box as all the other playboys I've met over my years, but that wasn't being fair to the man.

But something was wrong.

I've been feeling it the whole night, this tugging at the back of my mind that wanted my attention but couldn't fully come out. It's what woke me from my sleep. Soft light filters in from the bathroom where Everett had left the light on, and I realize for the first time in years, I forgot to switch on my nightlight. I was so tired it didn't even cross my mind.

The dark terrified me, I never forgot but I did tonight…

My brows tug low as confusion fogs my mind. What was it that I was missing? I didn't think much on the light, he probably just forgot to turn the light off before he came to bed but there was definitely something not quite adding up.

I roll onto my back and stare up at the ceiling, listening to the soft breathing next to me while my mind tries and fails to fully grasp the thought that initially woke me.

I play through the past twenty-four hours, starting from the minute I found Everett in the hotel and waking up just a moment ago. I replay every conversation, every minute of this interaction and then it clicks, and my heart gets lodged in my throat.

How did he know where I lived?

I didn't give him my address and it wasn't public knowledge.

My breathing starts to increase as panic overwhelms me. How did he know!? And then I'm thinking about the security panel, how it went down, and the convenient excuse made by the company. Could he have been here before? Did he know the code? The company?

Dear god, what did I just invite into my bed?

"Arryn," Everett's raspy voice sends fear straight through me. I scramble out of bed, darting for my robe to cover my naked body. I ached everywhere, was sore between my legs but I couldn't focus on that as Everett sits up slowly, glacial eyes narrowed on me. "Arryn."

"Who are you?" My voice comes out far steadier than I feel.

"What?"

"How did you know where I lived, Everett?"

He holds up his hand, "Arryn," He starts.

"Don't fucking lie to me either!" I snap loudly, "How. Did. You. Know."

I could feel my hands shaking, my heart pounding so hard behind my ribcage it felt like it was about to burst right out of my chest.

He remains quiet.

"Have you been here before?" I ask.

"Yes." He answers.

"Oh my god," I breathe, "Oh my *fucking* god!"

"Princess," He climbs out of bed, covered only by the white boxers he put on before we went to sleep. He was all hard muscle and honed perfection, a body that has been meticulously worked to be the best it could be. But he is littered with scars, old and new. They carve up his tan skin, silver, and pink marks in various shapes and sizes.

"Don't fucking *princess* me," I growl, reaching blindly behind me as if I could find something to defend myself with, "You're a fucking psycho!"

"I'm a lot of things," He replies in a calm and steady tone.

My fingers bump the ceramic pot I use to hold my makeup brushes and I grab it, emptying the contents all over the floor to wield it as a weapon.

"Now let's just calm down, shall we," He placates and that just enrages me further.

"You're a creep!" I launch the pot but don't stick

around to see if it hits him, instead I make a run for it, sprinting to the kitchen where I can grab a knife.

I slept with him! Fuck! What did I do!?

And here I was thinking this man wasn't like the rest.

Well, I guess he isn't. He is worse.

At least with the others I knew what to expect but with Everett I had no idea.

I should have listened to the warnings, shouldn't have ignored those blaring red flags.

"Arryn!" Everett yells but not in anger. I needed to find my phone, call the police but fuck if I could remember where I put it in my haste to get naked with Everett earlier. I grab a knife from the block and spin, finding Everett hastily putting on his clothes while he chases after me. He halts when he sees me brandishing the knife in his direction.

Pants hanging low from his narrow hips, shirt unbuttoned, he looks towards me without an ounce of fear or worry over the weapon. No, he just slides his hands into his pockets and cocks a brow.

"Look at you," He grins, eyes dropping down my body appreciatively, "So fucking beautiful when you're angry."

"Don't come any closer!" I warn him when he takes a step.

"Will you stab me?" He teases.

This fucker!

"Yes!"

"But we were so good together, princess," Everett purrs, "Put down the knife."

"Get the fuck out of my house."

"Let's not pretend you don't enjoy the risk," He says, circling me but keeping his distance, "You ignored those warning signs. You saw them, but I ended up here anyway."

"Did you con my father into working with you to get close to me?" I ask, "What do you do anyway?"

"No, I didn't," he says, and I believe him. Which means he saw me and decided I was his target. Perhaps it was just to get me into bed, he might not be dangerous per se but the moment the thought crosses my mind, I know it to be untrue. Everett was dangerous. "And I'm afraid I can't tell you right now what I do."

"Get out," I say, "Before I call the police."

He glances at the clock, "I'm coming back, little storm."

"No, you're not."

He grins, "We'll see."

He left hours ago but I couldn't stay in that house knowing he knew where I was. My gut was telling me he was behind the security issue even if I couldn't prove it. Why me? Why did it have to be me?

"Arryn," My father says, pulling at the collar of his shirt. A nervous tic he's had for as long as I have been scared of the dark. My mother's death did a number on all of us, and my father developed a serious case of anxiety and depression. He was better now, thanks to the medical professionals employed to help him but he showed the signs whenever he was under a lot of pressure. I didn't know what was on his plate at the moment to warrant this response, but I was also under a lot of stress right now.

"Well, where did you fucking find him?" I growl.

I couldn't outright say to my father what was happening since it would also reveal my night of soul shattering sex with the man, and while I had no qualms about sharing details about my sex life, sharing them with my father felt like a line I did not want to cross.

But if I could get more information about Everett, maybe I'll have more to go on to better defend myself against him.

"He's just a contact I am working with, Arryn, he won't be around for much longer."

"What business?" I press.

"It really doesn't matter," He tugs more furiously at the collar, "Now if you'll excuse me, honey, I have a business dinner to attend."

"Can I come?" I blurt.

"Really?"

"Yes! I mean yes," I fix the desperation in my tone, "Please, it would be nice to have an evening out of the house."

"Sure, honey, you can come."

CHAPTER NINE
everett

I've been following the two men for the past hour; they were in too much of a public place for me to take a good shot, so I've had to monitor and adjust the plan. I promised Victor the job would be complete today and it will be, it just has to be done at the right time.

I pull the car up outside the same restaurant they just stopped at, waiting a few minutes before I follow them inside. Hanging back, I watch them interact with the owner, talking in hushed tones which instantly gets my hackles up. This was the shadiest shit I've seen them do, but I suppose there could be blackmail and bribes being had that I don't know about.

The older of the two, Kenneth, shakes the owner's hand before he and his son head through to a table and take a seat. When the owner's back is turned, I sneak past him, heading through the door behind the front desk and down a narrow corridor, finding the small room they call an office where the security feed is running on the monitors.

I click through them until I find the camera that clearly shows the men's table, but something catches my eye, so I double up the screen.

Arryn is here. With Victor and another man.

They are in the private dining suite right behind where my two targets are sat. And that screams bad news.

This was no coincidence.

Arryn was pissed at me, but she'd forgive me, I'd make sure of it.

But this whole situation right here is making the hair on my neck stand on end. Wrong. It felt wrong.

I was raised to read rooms, people, and body language, I could tell someone's next move just by studying them for a few minutes and the men at the table had this strange sense of calmness to them, like they had settled on something and was ready to see it through.

I couldn't go in there and demand Arryn leave without exposing myself, and I couldn't take the men out in a dining room full of people without giving myself away. I'd gone this long without ever having a police tail, but if I were to be sloppy right now and remove the threat from Arryn, that's how this would end.

I keep both cameras up, watching the two of them as my targets eat and chat quietly, and Victor sells whatever the fuck he's selling to the single other man in the dining room with him. Arryn sits there quietly, chewing her lip until it's red, raw, and swollen. I hate that I've scared her. I could have lied when she asked me if I had been at her house before, but I didn't want to do that either.

About an hour passes when the restaurant starts to empty out, even the bar staff and wait staff leave until the only two people that remain are my targets and the three people in the room behind them. The owner clicks the lock on the entrance door and starts to head my way.

Shit.

I have no regrets when he walks through the door, and I jump before he can even set his eyes on my face. My hands frame his skull, and a quick, hard twist snaps his neck clean. He drops at my feet, lifeless, head twisted at an unnatural angle with vacant eyes staring up at the ceiling.

This fucker was clearly in on whatever my targets had planned and any threat against Arryn would be terminated without question.

My feet pound as I sprint down the hall, hand pulling out the Glock ready to defend, but the dining room is empty when I make it out.

"What are you doing here!?" I hear Victor shout before the tell-tale sound of a gun firing echoes through the building.

No.

"Arryn!" I roar at the same time she screams. It was the kind of sound that rips right through you, rattles your bones, and sets your teeth on edge.

I make it through the door to the sound of a second gun shot, watch as Victor's dinner guest goes down with a thud, head thumping off the edge of the table as he slumps to the floor, dead. And Arryn, she's fighting the son, trying to get away from him while he tries to wrap his hands around her throat.

"Hey!" I yell, lunging for him. Kenneth startles at my voice and fires blindly, hitting Arryn in the arm. She cries out, a wail of pain slicing through me. Sirens screech in the background, the shrill sound of it cutting through the room and I'm not the only one to hear it. Kenneth and Malakai spring into action, getting ready to flee. They scramble from the room, leaving the dead behind.

I should have chased them, ended them, but I don't. I go to Arryn as she slumps down the wall, going pale with a mix of shock and pain. Her father was dead, the second man also and she had watched it all happen.

"I've got you," I soothe.

Her eyes widen, "Get away from me!" She slurs, eyes hooded as fatigue tries to claim her.

"Stay awake, little storm!" I demand, "The police are almost here."

"I'll t-tell them," She stutters, "That you're a lunatic

stalker!"

"Hush, princess," I apply pressure to the wound on her arm, gritting my teeth when she cries out against the pain. The police are loud when they storm the restaurant.

"In here!" I yell. "Someone help! Call an ambulance!"

"Sir, move away!" One of the officer's orders.

"Can you tell me what happened?" Another says.

Arryn slumps against the wall, falling unconscious.

"Robbery," I tell them, "I was in the bathroom and came out to this." I lie.

"We have three dead," I hear someone say, "One injured."

I don't follow them to the hospital, as much as I wanted to check on Arryn, I had to eliminate the threat to her first. Except when I arrive at the Ware's address, it's dark and empty. I pull up the tracking I'd placed on their vehicles, seeing where it's currently located, and divert to their hotel a few blocks over from The Lauder hotel.

I locate the car, but my targets were nowhere to be found.

Shit. I try every tracker I have on them, but they all claim to be right here. If I couldn't see the tracker still on the bottom of the car, I would believe they'd found them and removed them. They had no idea I was on their tail, but they'd gone underground.

I'd overheard the cops before I'd left the restaurant, and they'd claimed the cameras had been wiped but they had a witness. Arryn.

Which meant she was their next target. I back out of the parking lot, hitting the gas as I speed onto the road, barely missing oncoming traffic in my attempt to get to the hospital. They're not going to wait around; they'll want her gone before she can speak to the cops and make a statement. Driving with one hand, I grab my cell from my pocket and load up the page where jobs are posted, hastily typing in her name.

"Shit!" I roar when her name pops up. Posted five minutes ago and it's already been claimed. The reward is half a million, which explains why it was accepted so quickly, but by *who*, I didn't know and couldn't see.

Either way, they were now a dead man.

Practically abandoning the car in front of the hospital, I rush inside, searching for a nurse to manipulate into giving me Arryn's room number. I find one and have the information in two minutes flat.

And it looks like I'm just in time. A dark figure is entering her room, cloaked in black, hands covered with leather gloves, he slips inside but I'm right behind him.

He's hovering over Arryn, facing the door so he sees

me as I enter. He has her IV in his hand, a syringe filled with a clear liquid in the other.

Motherfucker was about to overdose her.

"Drop it," I warn, reaching back for my gun.

"You shoot, we both go down," His eyes smile when his mouth doesn't. I don't recognize the hitman, though there had been an influx of new names suddenly available for hire and if this man was a rookie, scoring the kill on a name like Arryn Lauder would certainly boost his career.

"A chance I'm willing to take." I growl, stepping closer, "Now I'll give you two seconds to drop the fucking syringe and step away from my girl, before I put a bullet between your eyes and throw you out the goddamn window."

"You're Everett Avery," The guy cocks his head, "Huh, I thought you'd be bigger."

"One."

"Look man," the guy shrugs, "We all got to make a living." He says as he goes to plunge the syringe and let whatever drug loose into the tube that goes into Arryn's arm.

I lunge for him, managing to get him off before he's even pressed the syringe, forcing him back towards the wall of windows. I smash his head against the glass, once, twice, fighting him as he claws at me to try and escape, but on the fourth smash of his head the glass cracks as blood splatters. I use the weakness there and give a hard shove, forcing his body through the window, stepping away from fumbling hands as he tries to make purchase with something before he plunges to his death waiting six stories down.

I didn't have long now. Someone would have heard and if they hadn't, they'd soon find his body and trace it back to this room.

I glance to Arryn's sleeping form and pick up the syringe, breathing a sigh of relief when I see it still completely full and then go about unplugging her machines. By the looks of it, she is only on pain meds, a bandage on her arm from where the bullet had sliced through her. I pull the sheets back and slide my arms under her slumbering frame, hauling her to me and then I run.

And I keep running, only stopping once at my place to grab a few supplies and my equipment before I end up at the docks, phone in hand and calling my brother.

I was going back to the island, and I needed Torin's help.

CHAPTER TEN
everett

"The fuck is this!?" Torin growls, his anger twisting his features as he takes in the sleeping girl in my arms, still dressed in her hospital gown but now with my jacket covering her from the winter chill.

"We need to hide."

"Rett, you can't just go around kidnapping women!" He practically roars, "What did you give her!?"

"Now hold on, who said I gave her anything?"

Torin stares at me blankly.

"She's on pain meds, I haven't given her anything yet."

"*Yet!?*"

"Look, if we don't leave, she'll die, and the girl doesn't like me very much right now, so yes, I will sedate her if I need to."

"Fucking hell."

"Oh hush, brother," I roll my eyes at his dramatics, "She's just mad right now, she won't stay mad at me."

"And pray tell," Torin drawls, shaking his head, "Why is she mad at you?"

"Those are details you don't need to know."

"If I'm aiding you in kidnapping this poor girl, the least you can do is tell me what the fuck you did to put her life in danger."

"Why do you assume I had anything to do with it?"

He cocks a brow.

"Her father hired me," I snap, "To take out two targets, but the targets took out my employer before I got the chance to close the job. Now Arryn here has a hit on her head since she saw them do it."

"So, take out the employer?" Torin scoffs, "No employer, no payout."

"Can't, I lost them."

His laugh is loud in the quiet night, echoing through the empty docks where his boat idles in the water.

"Are you going to let us on or not?" I hiss.

He throws out an arm dramatically, "Hop on in."

I gently hand Arryn over to Torin, who takes her down to the single cabin below deck, as I grab the duffel from the car and jump onto the boat. Torin shakes his head at me, acting all fucking high and mighty like he has any right to think less of me for wanting to save the girl.

If it were Maya, his new wife, this would be a whole different story, and speaking of Maya...

"Don't tell Maya about this."

"Why not?"

"I don't need her riding me for the next god knows how long."

"My wife won't be riding anything," He growls.

I huff, "Jesus fuck, Tor, you ever gonna stop pissing on the girl? We get it, she's yours. This one," I jerk my chin to below deck, "is mine."

He grunts, reminding me of the long five years when my brother was a mere shell of himself.

"Does she know that?" He finally says.

"She will."

"Lord give me strength," Torin hisses in a breath before he begins to steer the boat away from the docks and the immediate danger. I settle onto the bench, breathing in the frosty sea air. It's pitch black out here on the water, the lights of the city and the docks mere blips on the horizon behind me, like earthbound stars but the sky... fuck the sky was beautiful. A black canvas full of bright white twinkling stars, the ocean somewhat calm considering the wind is blowing like a bitch, biting at my skin.

We're on the water for over an hour with only the sound of the ocean and the wind. Torin was focused on getting back to the small island and the tiny town of Ravenpeak Bay safely, and I was trying to come up with a plan to keep Arryn safe, while also trying to figure out how to handle the hit on her pretty little head.

Unfortunately, it wasn't as simple as getting it taken off. This only ended when she was dead.

And I wasn't going to let that happen.

"And just what do you expect to do from here, Everett?" Torin sighs, his back to me as he ties a rope, the boat bobbing idly on the water around the docks. Ravenpeak Bay is quiet this time of night, it's a sleepy town through and through, with its rustic charm and sprawling forests that climb the many peaks that act like sentinels around the island. And then there was the peak that gave this town its name, shaped like a raven, it overlooks the mouth of the bay like a protective God, watching the boats and the town beneath it.

"The cabin is still good," I heft the duffel onto the

dock, "It'll be a good spot to keep her until I can figure this shit out." I turn back to grab the rest of the supplies when I catch a glimpse of dark mused hair ascending the stairs, slow and clumsy but fuck, Arryn was awake an hour too damn soon.

"Shit!"

She reaches the deck, clinging to the narrow frame of the door and her wide, terrified eyes land on me right before she lets out an ear-splitting scream.

"What the fuck!" Torin curses.

I grab the syringe filled with the sedative and lunge for her, fighting off her scarily accurate punches aimed at my head considering the girl is still half dosed from all the pain meds. I manage to restrict her arms as she continues to wail before I plunge the needle into her neck.

"I'm sorry, little storm," The sedative is quick to take hold, slowing down her thrashing and relaxing her body, "I really didn't want to do that."

"I – I – I'm going – t – to–" She slumps, and I catch her before she can hit the ground, hoisting her into my arms.

"Kill me?" I finish what I assume she was going to say, "Yeah princess, I know."

Torin laughs, "Good luck brother, I ain't having shit to do with this."

"Fuck you, man!" I curse, maneuvering carefully out the boat and onto solid land, "I fucking helped you with Maya and now you're leaving me in the shit!? I fucking took a bullet for her and a damn coma, and this is how you repay me."

"For fucks sake," Torin grunts, "You're a real pain in my ass, you know that?"

"Just fucking get me up the peak to the cabin."

"It's still a thirty-minute trek, the other trails aren't big enough for the truck."

"Thirty minutes is better than two fucking hours, if not longer since it's dark."

"Wait here," He grunts and storms off before he returns with his truck. I lay Arryn down in the back seat, stealing a thick blanket from the cab to place over her before I launch the duffel and other bags into the bed. "You're not dressed to hike, Torin."

"I am not hiking."

"You damn well are, I can't carry her and the bags."

Torin grumbles like a grumpy old man the entire thirty minutes it takes us to hike from the truck he parked halfway up the only drivable trail leading up the peak. The cabin was in the deepest part of the woods, two hours on a direct path up the trail behind Torin's house. I'd had it built when we all discovered the island, but it's been practically abandoned these past five years.

It would need a deep clean and I'll use my leverage

on Torin some more to get him to bring me supplies. He was my older brother; I was allowed to manipulate him after I helped save his wife, and almost died in the process.

I get the cabin unlocked, fucking cold and tired but there was a lot to do before I could sleep. I needed to get Arryn warm, get this place straightened and try to explain to the girl exactly what's going on now.

Torin leaves the moment he can, reluctantly agreeing to bring me supplies in the morning.

After I settle Arryn into the bed in the only bedroom in the cabin, I cover her with a couple of blankets to get her warm again after the trek through the unforgiving winter chill, and go about getting a fire started to warm the place.

It was as bad as I thought it was going to be, dust everywhere, empty cupboards, cobwebs in the corners. But this was going to be home for the foreseeable future, and I needed to make it as such.

The last time I was in Ravenpeak Bay, I'd ignored this sense of calmness being out in the middle of nowhere brings. I'd ignored the pull to this cabin, a place I'd built for me for the quiet and the beauty of this small island, but now as I start to make the place more livable, the fat full moon penetrating through the holes in the trees, illuminating the fresh snow, I realize this is home.

Not the sterile apartment back on the mainland, nor the many other houses and apartments I have scattered across the US. This cabin, this one bedroom, log building surrounded by nothing but trees and rocks and snow, on this tiny island constantly battered by the elements and tormented by the rough sea, is *home*.

The island was like Arryn.

Wild. Beautiful. Unpredictable.

She reminded me of the storms and the skies, the unforgiving seas and wind. She was exactly as I call her. A storm. A *hurricane*.

So very fucking hard to ignore and harder not to be struck by the utter power and beauty of it.

She didn't even have to open her mouth for me to know she was a woman to worship.

CHAPTER ELEVEN
arryn

There's light streaming through a window where the curtains have been left open. I'm laying close to it, buried under a pile of blankets. I am fucking hot. Sweat slickens my skin and I hastily start to kick at them to try and get cool.

It takes me a moment to realize this is not the hospital. There are no beeping machines, instead the only noise I can hear is the caw of a raven – or maybe it was a crow, I didn't know the difference, and gone were the sterile walls and smell that was simply hospital, acidic, potent, and not at all comforting. But wherever I am now, smells delightful, like fresh wood burning on a fire, leather and pine. My arm twinges as I move to sit up, the stitches pulling like a bitch and the pain is a dull, throbbing ache that I choose to ignore as adrenaline spikes and my heart picks up speed.

So much had happened. My dad... *oh god, my dad!* Tears threaten as I recall the look of shock that crossed his face a moment before his body went limp. They'd shot him! Killed him. Right in front of me. It was like mom all over again, the blood, the screams, the panic... It was happening again.

I suck in a lungful of air and try to calm my breathing, just like the therapists told me to do when I went to them years ago.

I play through the memory, trying to detach myself from it so I can see it clearer without having my emotions jade what I can remember. It was a routine dinner, I didn't want to go home so I went with my dad, I was never supposed to be there. It was a normal fucking evening...until it wasn't.

I'd recognized them the moment they'd stormed the private dining room we had occupied for the evening. Kenneth and Malakai Ware were a growing thorn in my father's side. But they were just competition, they weren't supposed to be killers.

Or so I thought.

They hadn't hesitated when it came to shooting my father and the man he was having dinner with. It was Kenneth that pulled the trigger on the both of them, but it was Malakai who tried to pin me down so his dad could finish me off too.

There was so much blood. All over the floor, all over

me. And while I could detach myself somewhat, it didn't stop the older memories from layering on top of the new ones.

I choke on my own sob, hand coming around my throat as if it could stop the lump forming, threatening to choke me as flashbacks of the night my mother died play through my mind. The memories of the night when she was murdered.

It was so dark, my father and I had gone out with my sister for the evening, my mother wasn't feeling well so she stayed home. We lived in a safe neighborhood, nothing bad had ever happened there. We got back late, and I was the first one through the door, I was so used to walking in late and not wanting to disturb anyone, I left the lights off. I could navigate that house with my eyes closed so I didn't need it and that night was no different. I kicked my shoes off at the door and stepped through to what was the living room, but then my foot hit a thick wet patch on the wood flooring, and I slipped. I cried out as my head thumped off the floor but then I noticed how wet it was, it was soaking through my clothes, it was on my skin and hands and face.

"Dad!" I'd called, wincing with the throb in my head, "Dad, I think there's a leak!"

I heard both my dad and my sister rush in, I was still trying to get up off the floor, trying not to slip again and then the lights were turned on and I had to shield my eyes against the burn.

My sister screamed. It was the kind of sound that you

remember years later, in the dead of night when everything else is silent. It's the kind of sound that rattles your bones and sinks into the very soul of you, marking you from inside. When I finally looked at them, my sister was sobbing, clutching her mouth as if it could contain the cries she was unleashing, but my dad was staring at me. My eyes dropped to my hands and then I saw it.

The blood.

I was covered in blood. I was wearing white that night, but it was stained red, my skin was smeared with it, it was under my nails.

I swung around and found her immediately.

My mother.

I didn't know a person could bleed so much. I guess I never really thought about it. But I'd come in and slipped on her blood, landed only a foot away from her still and lifeless corpse.

Every night after that, whenever I turned the lights off, I would have flashbacks, feel the blood on my skin and I'd wake up screaming. So, I stopped turning the lights off.

And have done that ever since.

My father's blood had splattered across my face when he was shot and shakily, I look down at my hands, finding rusty stains under my nails. I have to swallow down the need to vomit. I needed to take stock of my surroundings, figure out where I was and how I got here.

Had the Ware's come and taken me? I remember a boat.

It rocked under my feet when I tried to stand up after waking in the tiniest room I'd ever been in. The bed was narrow, and the sheets were scratching and god, the smell was fucking awful. Like fish, salt and metal.

I'd gripped whatever I could reach and made my way to a narrow set of steps and hauled myself up them, confused and dazed, and when I reached the top, I was hit in the face by bitter cold air, the wind whipping at my hair and trying to topple me back down the stairs.

And then I saw him.

Everett fucking Avery.

He was there at the restaurant too and on the boat. He was the source of every nightmare of recent. And he'd lunged at me, stabbing something into my neck. The fatigue had taken purchase immediately after whatever drug he'd just forced into me, and he'd knocked me out again.

And now I am here.

He kidnapped me.

Everett kidnapped me.

Oh. My. God.

I needed to stay calm but that was really fucking hard when I had no idea where I was, and a goddamn *madman* had kidnapped me. I was still in my hospital gown; the drugs were still wreaking havoc on my system, and I didn't know where he was.

Was he here? If I opened this door, is he going to be waiting for me?

Slowly, I sit up and place one leg on the floor, trying to keep it as light as I can. I didn't want to stand on any creaky floorboards that could make him aware that I'm awake but once both feet are on the floor, I sweep my gaze around the room. It's all wood, log walls with some minimalistic artwork of dramatic cliffsides and stormy seas.

The bed is a small double, with piles of blankets and pillows. A single dresser with drawers and a mirror is up against one wall, and a wardrobe to match sits close by. There's space for a person to stand width ways around every side of the bed but not much more than that. I creep to the window, slow, steady, quiet, and peak outside to find trees and snow and that's all.

Just miles and miles of pines that stretch into a grey sky that is unleashing more snow. It appeared we were on some kind of slope and grey, sharp rocks jut out from the blanket of white on the ground but there was no real way to determine how deep the snow was.

I try to open the window but find it stiff with age, unable to open more than a few inches but with that small crack, sound filters in and the first thing I hear is the unmistakable sound of waves crashing on rocks.

Closing the window as softly as I can, I turn back and head to the door, pressing my ear to it but when I hear nothing from the other side, I decide to open it just a small amount.

I can hear a coffee machine immediately, making a fresh cup and the sizzle of something cooking in a pan.

I wasn't alone.

I brave opening it some more to peer out into the hall. Wherever we were was small enough that I could see all the way to the front door. The walls blocked whatever was before that, but I assumed it was a kitchen and living area.

There were no creaky floorboards so far, and mixed in with the smell of bacon and coffee was the distinct aroma of cleaning products and logs burning. Creeping towards that noise and smell, I instantly freeze when I see his back.

Shirtless with just a pair of grey sweats hanging from his narrow hips, he's facing away from me, hands working over the stove as he cooks. I do a sweep of the room, the kitchen counter is littered with fruit, bread, pots and pans, a disarray of different things all mashed together as if someone had upturned several bags all at the same time. But I was eyeing that heavy looking iron skillet, still brand new with the sticky label right in the middle of it.

I lunge for it, wrapping my hand firmly around the handle but the rest of the items clatter to the floor, eggs cracking open and grapes rolling.

Everett twists around to me at the same time I swing, the skillet hitting him across the cheek. He twists and hits the counter, going down hard and I don't think, I just run.

I keep the pan as my weapon of choice, leaping into the snow, the cold and wet not even registering as adrenaline propels me forward.

Instinct told me I needed to go down, I just had to battle this snow to do so, and it was *thick*. It came up to just below my knees, some spots even higher and I'm drenched in icy water in no time, skin reddening as the ice bites at my body, melting into freezing water that soaks my clothes and numbs my toes.

But I keep going. I keep battling because the other option was to go back to that cabin with the man that kidnapped me. The man that clearly has some part to play in my father's murder.

My fingers keep a tight grip on the skillet, the joints in my hands aching with how tight I hold it, and my skin starts to sting with the cold but still, I move.

Even when I hear him roar my name behind me.

CHAPTER TWELVE
everett

"Fuck!" I grunt, rubbing the spot on my cheekbone that currently feels like it's on fire. She hit me fucking good with that skillet, so props to her for using a damn kitchen utensil as a weapon. The woman has one hell of a swing on her. I could feel blood trickling down the side of my face from where the impact of the hit had split the skin and I knew there was going to be a bruise there, but my cheekbone didn't feel broken even if it felt like it was trying to push its way out of my face.

I'd gone unconscious for a few seconds and by the time I'd woken, she was gone, the front door left wide open. Snow was currently building up on the floor just inside the door.

I shake my head trying to clear the lingering fog and stumble after her. She was just in a damn hospital gown, though I wasn't wearing much more than she was as I stumble through the fresh tracks left by her lithe body. I could see her dark mane of hair, a stark contrast to the pristine white snow as she tries to flee down the cliff.

I was surprised she was going the right way to be honest, but in this weather and dressed like that, neither of us would survive thirty minutes out here.

"Arryn!" I roar her name, the sound of my voice bouncing off the trees and sending a flock of ravens soaring into the grey skies. She tries to run faster but even in this weather, I was quicker. "Arryn, stop!"

"Get away from me!" She screeches back, tripping and falling face first into the snow. She lets out a frustrated scream and tries to get moving again, but I'm already on her. I won't lie, chasing her through the woods is doing something to me. I grab her around the waist and haul her back against my chest, avoiding her flailing arms and legs as she tries to land a hit on me.

"Let me go!" She swings the hand around still holding that damn skillet and smacks it into my knee. I grunt but don't let go.

"Stop fucking fighting!" I growl.

"I'm going to fucking shove this pan up your ass if you don't let me go!" She warns.

But it just makes me laugh, the chase, the fight, all of it shooting blood straight to my cock.

"Are you fucking hard right now!?" She screeches, "You're a psycho!"

I spin us quickly, forcing her back into the snow and land on top of her.

"I'm going to make it real fucking clear, little storm," I growl, nose to nose with her. I have her wrists in my hands, pinning them down and her body beneath mine, legs split so I'm within the cradle of her thighs, "The nearest town to here is a two-hour trek on a good day, in this weather you're looking at four hours, if not more. It gets dark early, and if you think it's cold now, wait until night falls. You'll never make it to the town before you freeze to death, and if that doesn't happen, do you want to come face to face with a fucking bear or bobcat? Because I can tell you now, princess, that skillet will only do so much at protecting you against a predator."

Her stormy eyes bounce between mine as if searching for the lie in my words. While bears here are rarely seen, it doesn't mean they're not here and I damn well knew there were bobcats in these woods as well as god knows what else. She'd never survive.

"Served me fine against *you*."

I grin down at her, and she tilts her chin up in defiance. I was sat so fucking perfectly between her legs, I could grind forward right now and feel her heat against me, but I don't. I'd have her again but preferably when she isn't trying to actively kill me. She'll likely keep trying to kill me but right now we were both cold, shivering and going numb. We needed to get back to the cabin and warm up.

"I was distracted," I tell her, "You won't be so lucky next time. Now are you going to behave so we both don't freeze to death?"

"No!" She shouts defiantly.

"For fuck's sake, princess," I roll my eyes and use my weight and training against her, disarming her of the pan quickly before I hoist her up and over my shoulder. It wasn't easy, not when she's thrashing and hitting me as I try to climb the incline back towards the cabin. It was only a short distance, but my feet were numb, fingers numb, and goddamn it was fucking cold.

I manage to get us to the cabin some fifteen minutes later, her fight lagging but she still tries to get away from me. I kick the door closed and dump her ass on the couch, the fire still burning but slower since I needed to add more wood. It is warm though and it instantly starts to thaw the chill on our skin.

"Take off your gown," I order.

"Fuck you."

"You want me to do it for you?" I cock a brow and let my eyes drop down her body. "I will, princess. You need to get out of these wet clothes and warm up and I have no problem aiding you."

"I hate you."

"No, you don't," I head to the bags by the door and pull out a pair of my sweats and a t-shirt, throwing them onto the couch beside her, "You just don't understand right now."

"Don't tell me what you think I know; I *know* I hate you. You kidnapped me! My dad fucking died," she chokes, "And you took me! Oh my god. No one will find me here."

"That's the idea, Arryn, this is the only place you're safe."

"*Safe!?*" She shrieks.

"Get changed, Arryn. I'll make breakfast."

"Is it drugged?" She sneers at my back.

"If you keep with this damn attitude," I throw over my shoulder, "It will be."

I hear her stomp like an angry child to the bathroom and then she slams and locks the door. I knew the window in there was too small for her to climb through, so I don't go and demand she leaves it open and get on with getting changed myself, and then finish up the breakfast I'd started before the tussle in the snow. The shower turns on a moment later, the old pipes in the cabin sputtering to life as the water heats, but then five minutes pass, ten and then fifteen and she still isn't out.

The breakfast is plated, the coffee brewed and on the small oak table, but she's still in the shower.

I wipe my hands on a towel as I cross the short space and rap my knuckles on the door, "Arryn?"

"Fuck off!" She snaps.

Whistling as I walk away from the door, I head to the

kitchen sink and twist the cold tap on to full, waiting a few seconds before –

A shrill scream echoes through the cabin as cold water rushes out of the shower head.

The door flies open a moment later and Arryn, burning red with her anger storms towards me, "You fucking asshole!" She swings a fist.

"So fucking violent, princess," I grab her wrist before her hand ever makes contact and have her pinned under me on the sofa in the next second.

Her towel falls open, bearing her perfectly delectable body, all toned muscles, and curves to sink my teeth into.

"I have to warn you, your fight turns me on." I let my eyes lick down her body where it's pinned beneath mine. "It kinda feels like flirting. Are you flirting with me princess? You don't need to go to so much trouble, I'm yours."

Her breath saws from her lungs as her jaw pops with how hard she is gritting her teeth. "It's okay," I muse, letting myself closer, close enough I can bury my face into the side of her neck, "You're allowed to react to me." I say, feeling the heels of her feet pressing into my ass but not kicking, instead is pulling me closer. Her warm pussy presses into my hard cock and I grind forward.

She lets out a shocked gasp, tilting her face to the side as I lick up the column of her throat, "Keep this violence, little storm, keep your fight."

"Get off me," She groans.

She wraps her legs around my waist, a complete contradiction to her demand for me to get off, and presses herself up and against the aching length behind my sweats.

I just about lose a couple of brain cells with how good it feels. Her hands slide up my back and then into my hair as she tugs on the strands. And then in the next minute, I'm on my fucking back on the floor in front of the couch, and her very naked body is straddling mine.

She glares down at me, chest heaving, nipples peaked and chest beautifully flushed. My hands land on her thighs and I give them a squeeze, the flesh yielding beneath my unforgiving grip.

She leans towards me, grinding herself over my length and my mouth parts. Fuck, I wanted to be inside this woman. Now.

Her nose touches mines, lips a barely there whisper against my mouth, "If you think for one fucking minute, Everett Avery, that I'll let you touch me like that again, then I worry I hit you hard enough to cause damage. I can assure you, you'll never fucking have me again."

I laugh against her mouth, licking my tongue against the seam of her lips, "Is that right, princess?"

"Yes," She hisses.

"Then why are you grinding your wet little cunt all over my cock?"

CHAPTER THIRTEEN
everett

She clambers off me so quickly you'd think my ass was on fire and then snatches up the towel from the couch, wrapping it back around herself as she glares at me.

"Just for the record," she hisses with enough venom to rival a viper, "I wasn't fucking wet. Around you I'm drier than the Sahara Desert."

"You keep telling yourself that, princess," I call to her retreating form, "This wet spot on my sweats tells me otherwise."

"I just got out of the shower!" She argues.

"Tell whatever excuse you need to, to be able to sleep

at night. We both know the truth."

"And what truth is that, Everett?" She stops at the bathroom door and spins towards me.

"That you want me regardless of what you know. Don't worry, princess. I'm a patient man, I can wait. But can you?"

"Asshole," She mutters to herself as she closes the bathroom door.

Her fork scrapes across the plate as she moves the same piece of bacon from one side to the other for the hundredth time.

"You have to eat." I mutter.

"Why are you doing this?" She drops the fork and levels me with her glacial stare.

"Because I am keeping you safe, princess."

"From what?" She snaps.

"Your father…" I sigh, "He died."

"I am aware," Her voice comes out thick as if fighting a lump in her throat, "He was murdered. Did you have something to do with that!?"

"I was working *with* your father, not against him."

I didn't know how much to tell her; did I want to mar whatever image she had of Victor? Did she know what he was up to behind those office doors? I was guessing not.

"And you happened to be there at the same time he died?" She crosses her arms, wincing, "It's funny how you just show up, oh wait," she clicks her fingers, feigning surprise, "You were following me. That's right, you're a damn stalker so I shouldn't be surprised you were there, right?"

"Funnily enough, Arryn, I wasn't there for you, but it was a *delightful* surprise."

"Delightful?" She twists her mouth in disgust, "My father and another man are dead, and you think this situation is delightful?"

"There is beauty in death, princess. Let's not forget that."

"There is nothing beautiful about this, Everett. You're a sick man. Get help."

She doesn't wait for me to respond; she gets up from the table and shuts herself in the bedroom. With a sigh I drop my head into my hands, rubbing at the tension headache I feel blooming behind my eyes.

She was stubborn, bratty, and angry. There would be no getting through to her right now. She still had to process her dad's death, still had to grieve and on top of that, I had to explain why exactly I brought her here.

Sure, I was selfish in most of my reasoning, but I *was* trying to keep her safe.

No one would look for her here. No one would suspect I took her.

And until I could figure out how to remove the hit from her head, this would be where she remained.

The Wares are smart, I'd checked every few hours looking for a trace of them, but they'd remained silent and invisible since the attack at the restaurant. I had to wonder what connections they had to pull that off, who they had in their pockets to keep their records clean that not even I, could see that coming.

They didn't look like killers and yet I was proven wrong and that very rarely happens.

I log into my computer an hour later, checking the open hit on Arryn's head. Another guy had accepted the job after the last one was found dead and the clock for him was running out. That was standard on these kinds of hits, a week to get the job done and proof of completion before any money is paid and this guy had five days, twelve hours and exactly six minutes to complete before someone else can try their hand.

I didn't know who Arryn's current hitman was, that information wasn't freely available on this database, since, according to the organizations rules, it could jeopardize their mission if another wanted the job and had lost out.

The men and women who worked like this were ruthless, and not one of us were afraid of taking out the competition if it meant a hefty paycheck at the end of it.

My brothers and I had worked for the organization for

a long time, trained by our own father, who was one of the best in the game before his own death. Torin retired a little over five years ago, Kolten, our adoptive brother has been AWOL for God knows how long, and then there's me who will likely never leave the game.

Picking up my phone, I step outside and dial my brother.

"She hasn't murdered your ass yet, then?" Torin answers with a laugh.

"How did you make Maya fall in love with you?"

"What?" His laughter only increases.

"Well, it wasn't your sunshiny personality, was it," I grumble, "You're grumpier than a hungry bear."

"I didn't *make* Maya do anything."

"Okay but what did you do?"

"Nothing, Everett, it just happened."

I grunt but don't say anything in return.

"I assume your first day isn't going as well as you hoped." I could hear the amusement in his voice, and I knew he was just eating this up. "Surely you didn't expect her to thank you for kidnapping her."

"I didn't kidnap her."

"What do you call it?"

"Relocating her until I can figure out how to keep her

safe."

"That's kidnap."

"Yes well, it was either this or letting her die. What would you have me do?"

He sighs, "I don't know Rett, but you can't just expect the girl to forgive what you did."

When I don't say anything else he continues.

"Why don't you actually *try* with her. Like I don't know, do something she likes. You've taken her from her life, Everett, you need to give a little. And if there's anything I've learned, brother, is that lying will cost you. Tell her the truth."

I didn't know how I was going to do that when she has locked herself away and was trying to maim me every chance she got. I agree and then hang up, stepping back into the warmth of the cabin.

She doesn't come out of the room at all. I stoke the fire, make her coffee, and bring her water but she only opens the door once she knows I'm gone.

Now the sun has set, and silence has fallen on the cabin, darkening the woods around us.

The door to the bedroom squeaks open, "Everett?"

"In here," I call out.

Her bare feet pad through to where I'm sat at the kitchen table, the laptop open in front of me which I close at her arrival.

"Can you tell me?"

I scan her face, noting the puffy, red rimmed eyes and pink cheeks. She's been crying. Silently. Alone.

"Tell you what?"

"Why they did it?"

I think back to my brothers' words only a few hours ago. I could lie, tell her I don't know and keep whatever image she has of her father clean but if I had any hope of her understanding…

"I can."

"Are you going to lie?" She narrows her eyes at me.

"Sit down, princess." I order gently, "I'll tell you."

glass impatiently.

"Your father contacted me for a certain set of skills I possess."

I feel my jaw twitch as I clench it in irritation at the cryptic way he's speaking with me.

"Spit it out."

"I'm trying here, princess, how about you stop being a brat."

"Wow." I scoff, "you're an asshole. You think I want to be here, sitting here at this stupid fucking table with a madman?"

"I'm not mad."

"Could've fooled me, Everett."

He didn't deserve an ounce of kindness from me. I could think he was attractive. I knew what he could do to my body, how he could make me feel and those memories, of course, were going to make me react. It was hard to forget something like that when no one has ever made me feel the way he did, but he was still an asshole.

"For fuck's sake, Arryn, I kill people. He hired me as a fucking hitman!"

My blood turns to ice right there in my veins.

"I am a hired killer, Arryn, and I was working on a double hit with your dad before he died."

"Who?" I whisper, throat closing around the word.

"Kenneth and Malakai Ware."

I choke on the air in my lungs. "No. No, you're wrong."

He sighs and drags a laptop closer, typing something on it before he spins it and shows me the screen.

It was a wire transfer, from my dad to Everett for quarter of a million dollars. "Half of my fee, paid a week before I was due to take out the targets."

My eyes flick to the date on the transfer, "A week has already passed."

"I was preparing for the hit the night they killed your father."

"They did it because my dad was going to do it to them?"

"I don't know, princess. But whatever reason they had; I will find it out. Your father did it to eliminate the competition, perhaps they thought the same."

I stare down into the glass. My father never spoke to me about the stress he was facing with the Ware's setting up and growing damn quick in the city. My father has owned the Lauder Hotel and Resort chain for a long time, and I knew the Wares were stepping in on some of that clientele that kept it running but I didn't think it was *that* bad. To put a kill hit on the competition? No, I couldn't believe it. My dad would never hurt –

"I see your thoughts, little storm. This is not a lie."

"And I'm supposed to believe you?" I stand up abruptly. "You're a killer, Everett. You have a bank full of blood money, you *stalked* me, *kidnapped* me, and I'm just supposed to believe what you're saying. I know my dad; he wouldn't do this!"

"You know I'm telling the truth, but you're too caught up in what you think you know, to believe it right now."

"I want to go home."

"I can't do that, princess."

"And why not!?"

"Because you're next."

"Excuse me!?"

"You witnessed it, Arryn, and believe it or not, I did not have any intention of bringing you here but when I got to you, there was someone already there ready to murder you right in your hospital bed."

"And what, you're my knight in shining armor? Should I be thanking you now?"

He stares blankly at me.

"So, make it go away," I snap, "You're a big bad assassin, right. Make it go away."

"It's not that simple."

"Why not?"

"Because they put your hit on a database, open to everyone to claim. It doesn't come down until they prove you're dead."

I was really good at hiding the fear that was pumping through my body. My heart was pounding, the skin on my back slick with perspiration and my mind whirling through the information I've just been given.

"So, I can never go back?" I do my best to hide the tremor in my voice, but I know he hears it. His icy eyes soften, and he gently closes the laptop.

"Arryn," He starts.

"No!" I frantically step away, overwhelmed by just about everything.

"Princess, breathe."

"Stay away from me, Everett. *Stay away from me!*"

He stops his advance as I back my way towards the bedroom. I asked for answers, he gave me them, but I didn't like these answers. I didn't like this truth if it was even that. He could be lying.

He *was* lying. He had to be.

He opens his mouth to speak but I bolt, slamming the door to the bedroom closed as I frantically move to the only large piece of furniture in here. The wooden dresser is heavier than I expected but I manage it, even if I pull a muscle doing it as I push it in front of the door.

I was getting the fuck out of here and Everett wasn't

going to stop me.

CHAPTER FIFTEEN
everett

It's around day three when Arryn stops physically trying to maim me. The girl was ruthless in her attempts, I would give her that and everything in this tiny little cabin was a weapon. I'd had to hide all the sharp objects from her since I didn't much like the idea of being impaled by the fire poker.

She'd hid for half a day after I'd told her about the hit, pushed the dresser in front of the door and attempted to smash a window but I'd caught her and after threatening to take the door off the hinges she stopped.

I felt like I was dealing with a bratty teenager after they'd been grounded, except this was a full-grown woman and she was stubborn as all hell.

"Eat," I grunt, dropping the plate of food in front of

her. She glares at me but picks up the fork and I go to the fire, adding more logs to keep it burning and warming this place.

The snow hadn't stopped in three days, it was just white outside the windows and bitterly cold. It was actually a good thing. While I didn't believe anyone would find us here, if they did, it would be tough for just about anyone to climb this peak during this snowstorm. But it did mean we were trapped here until it cleared some. I'd contacted Torin but there was no way any supplies were reaching us until the snow at least stopped falling in torrents.

I'd been keeping a close eye on the file for Arryn, it had yet to tick over to the next hitman since the current one still had a couple of days and even though I had tried to get information through some of my most trusted sources, no one had the information I wanted.

The Wares were still hiding.

When Arryn has cleared her plate and gone off to sulk in front of the fire, watching the snow fall peacefully outside the window, I take a moment to watch her.

So many different puzzle pieces to fit together. She was all sharp edges and venom, her defenses built so high and violently, it was hard to see what was underneath.

But in times like this, when the cabin is quiet, and she isn't actively trying to murder me, I can see a side of softness to her she doesn't show anyone. She doesn't like to be vulnerable, I've realized, in front of anyone, but I could see the way her shoulders loosen and her pretty lips part on a sigh, she is somewhat enjoying the serenity this cabin has to offer.

"The TV is old," I say, clearing the kitchen and taking a few small steps towards her, "but it should get a signal and work, though I doubt there's many channels to choose from."

Her eyes bounce to mine before they do a sweep of my body. I was in sweats again today. I couldn't remember the last time I'd gone this long without putting on a suit.

She thinks I don't notice when she looks at me like that, when her eyes heat and a small pink bloom of color highlights her cheeks, as if she is remembering the night we shared barely a week ago, before everything went to shit.

She averts her eyes and reaches for the ancient-looking remote, pressing the button to turn on the TV. Static greets her but after a few button presses she finds a live channel. It's just a news channel but she settles into the cushions, pretending to be enraptured by the current story playing on the screen about some new property developments happening on the East coast.

I leave her to it until I hear a gasp from her.

"It's been almost a week since heiress and model, Arryn Lauder was reported missing. This story comes after her father, Victor Lauder, was found dead at a restaurant in central Portland, Maine. Authorities believe his death follows a string of robberies targeting the dining and hospitality sector of the city. Arryn's sister, Olivia has released a statement with regards to her sister's disappearance."

"Arryn," I reach for the remote in her hand.

"No!" She cries, "Let me watch."

The camera cuts to a prerecording of Olivia Lauder standing outside of the Lauder hotel. The young girl's eyes are puffy and red rimmed from tears. She looks ill, with the dark shadows under her eyes and the pale complexion of her skin.

"Please," She starts, her voice cracking on that simple word. Arryn's hand flies to her mouth, eyes glued to the TV as her sister pleas to the camera for any news about her sister, "If anyone, anyone at all, has any information about my sister, Arryn, hand it over to the police. She doesn't deserve this."

Arryn jumps when my hand lands on her shoulder, but she doesn't shove me off which I expected her to do. Instead, she accepts the small amount of comfort I can offer her.

"She would want to say goodbye to our father." Olivia continues, "If you know anything, call the number on the screen now and help bring my sister home."

"Can't you do something?" Arryn whispers, "Send a tip to them that I'm safe?"

"I can't do that," I tell her softly, "I can't risk anyone finding you."

"But how would they!?" She snaps, "If you do it

anonymously?"

"Because it doesn't work that way, princess, if the people after you get hold of the information, there are plenty of ways to trace the tip back. They would find you. Is that what you want?" She tries to pull away from me, but I don't let her. I round the couch and grab her chin, not hard but firmly, forcing her to look at me with her hate filled gaze, "They find you Arryn and it won't just be your father your sister is burying, it *will* be you too."

"Why the fuck do you care!?"

"Because I fucking do!" I growl, "Because regardless of how long I have known you, you deserve a long and fucking happy life. And if I have to keep you safe for the rest of your fucking life, I will. Because I have taken responsibility for that damn heart inside of your chest and I will do all I damn well can to keep it beating for as long as I can!"

"I'll get a bodyguard." She again tries to snatch away from me.

"No one can protect you better than I can." I whisper, leaning in closer, "No one will stand between you and what's after you."

Her eyes bounce between mine, wide and filled with emotion that no matter how hard she tries to hide, she can't.

"There is no one better for you than me, little storm."

Her lips part and her breath fans against my mouth as the TV continues to play behind me, already moved onto a new story about some dog sanctuary halfway across the country.

"You already know that don't you princess? There is no one more perfect for you than me."

"I don't even like you," she whispers.

I chuckle, "So you keep saying, but I'm certain those are just pretty lies. You just hate that you can't hate me."

"How do you figure that?" Her tongue traces her plump bottom lip as her eyes drop to my mouth.

"Because I'm the only man you've been with that can play this body like an expert musician. I am the only man willing to let you be who you are supposed to be. I don't want to squash all this power or dim who you are supposed to be. You're not a pretty little woman to be on an arm, you're a woman who should lead a fucking army. And I just want to witness it."

I lean just a little closer, my lips a whisper against hers, the touch soothing an itch I haven't been able to scratch, "You're no trophy, Arryn. You don't belong behind glass walls for everyone to look at. Fight me all you like, princess, I like it when you're a little violent but let's not pretend you fucking hate me. You hate what I've done and that's fair, but you don't hate me."

"I do."

I grin as I let my mouth firmly rest against hers, waiting for the slap or punch but it doesn't come.

I test the limit by letting my tongue run across the seam of her mouth and when she parts for me, I waste no time in deepening the kiss. I fist a handful of her hair, tugging until she follows my lead and angles her head, letting me in further. She moans into my mouth, the taste of her so damn sweet on my tongue.

One hand still tangled in her hair, I drop the other to the soft curve of her waist, letting my fingers sink into her flesh as I yank her forward, pressing every hard inch of my body into every part of hers. I capture her gasp in my mouth, forcing her backwards until the backs of her knees hit the edge of the couch and then guide her down, her legs parting to let me in as I cover her and kiss her until I'm an inch away from going feral.

The TV cuts to a commercial and sudden blaring music jolts both of us. Her teeth suddenly sink into my lip, hard, drawing blood.

"Fuck!" I yell, pulling away from her.

"Don't ever touch me again!" She growls fiercely.

I swipe the blood from my lip with my tongue, my blood molten in my veins and don't get me started on how hard my damn cock is.

Rolling my head side to side, I readjust myself in my sweats, looking down at where she remains sprawled on the couch. Her chest heaves and her skin is flushed and there's no real heat behind her glare.

"Come find me when you can't take the ache anymore, princess. I'm going to take a fucking cold shower."

"Asshole!" Is her reply.

CHAPTER SIXTEEN
everett

I never used to have a problem using my hand. A quick jerk off in the shower was enough but since I'd had a taste of that little fucking hurricane, my cock in my hand wasn't sufficing.

I rest one hand on the tiles of the shower wall, the other pumps up and down the aching shaft of my dick. And it was right fucking there, the release but it just wouldn't happen. "Fuck!" I growl, dropping my hand, my cock aching and still damn hard.

I shut off the shower and wrap a towel around myself, throwing open the bathroom door to find Arryn on the couch, curled under a blanket with a packet of cookies on her lap. She throws a seething glare over her shoulder which abruptly falls flat as her eyes take in the water dripping down my chest and the tent I'm pitching at the front of the towel.

"Unless you're planning on getting on your fucking knees and dealing with it, princess, I suggest you stop staring at it."

Her mouth drops open.

"Yeah, something like that," I comment, grabbing fresh clothes from the bag since I'd forgotten to take them into the bathroom with me, "But just over here and on your knees." I point to the floor.

"Pig," She grunts, turning her attention back to the TV.

I don't bother going back to the bathroom to change, I drop the towel and step into the fresh pair of boxers and then the pants. "I'm impressed you didn't try to escape."

"I did." She shrugs, stuffing a cookie into her mouth and concentrating on the TV real hard. "Shame those six fucking locks got in the way. Overkill much?"

"Well, I figured one wouldn't hold you, and two didn't seem like much," I grab mugs from the cupboard to make coffee, "six seemed like a good number."

"You can't just keep me in a cage, Everett."

I roll my eyes, "This again, princess?"

"Stop calling me princess, it's demeaning."

"No can do, princess," I chuckle at her dramatic sigh.

"Coffee?"

"Sure."

We are somewhat civil for the next hour; I supposed the wall of blankets Arryn built between us on the couch helped. She did offer me a cookie though, so, you know, *progress*.

"Are there warmer clothes in that bag?" She asks, placing the remote down.

"Are you cold?"

"A little." She was in my sweats and one of my t-shirts, the fire was burning hot and healthy in the burner, but the snow was still coming down thick and heavy outside the window.

"There's a couple of my sweatshirts in there," I tell her, "Help yourself."

She gives me a barely there smile and stands before going over to the bag, rummaging through the clothes in there and then locks herself in the bathroom.

I switch the TV off, stretching out on the couch. It was getting late, the light outside dimming as the sun begins to set on this peak and the tiny little town at the bottom. I use the time Arryn's in the bathroom to run the checks again on my laptop, finding nothing new since this morning. I do a quick scan of the open job list, Arryn's hit still open on a second tab. If I wasn't here, I'd be on a number of these jobs, cashing in on those hefty checks promised. But since the coma a few months back and the girl I took care of, I hadn't hit anyone in a long time.

It was an itch under the skin somedays and a burning craving the next.

When you're raised to be good at one thing and it's the only thing you know, it becomes the air you breathe. Going without was like going through a withdrawal. The rush. The adrenaline. It's like a shot straight into the veins. You become addicted to the high of it, the rush of power and control.

Completing jobs gave me a purpose. It was what I was born for.

I made a lot of questionable choices. Did a lot of questionable things and toed the line of bad and evil like it was a skipping rope, and I was teasing the devil.

But I suppose, if I was to be tied up doing something else, this right here was the perfect distraction.

There's a sudden loud thump from the bathroom and I get up quickly, knocking the chair back, "Arryn!?" I slam a fist on the door, reaching around the counter for the gun I have stashed to the underside.

"I'm good!" She calls back breathlessly.

"What are you doing?"

"Nothing!"

My suspicion rises at the haste in which she answers,

"I'm coming in."

"Don't you dare!"

"Either unlock the door or I'll break it down."

"Everett, do not come in here!" She yells. The shower was still running, and I could hear this knocking sound accompanied by her grunts. What the fuck was she doing in there?

"I'll count to three, princess," I warn, "if you haven't answered the door by three, I'm knocking this damn door down."

"Everett!" She yells.

"One."

"Do not!"

"Two."

"Fuck!" She cries, "Ow!"

"Three."

I ram my shoulder into the door, once, twice, the old creaky wood groaning under the pressure. It splinters on the third and opens right up on the fourth.

I barge through, expecting to find her fallen in the shower or on the floor but instead I find…

Her ass sticking out the window, the upper half of her body lodged in the tiny window frame.

I knew she wouldn't fit, which was why I hadn't worried about her escaping out of it. But clearly this woman had no perception of space.

"Get out!" She screams.

An icy chill is slipping in through the tiny gaps at the top, but it appears she's stuck around her hip area. The shower was running but she hadn't gotten in it. The time she'd spent in the bathroom was used in this foiled attempt at escape.

She wiggles trying to free herself but for whatever reason she can't back out.

"Did you really look at the window and think you'd fit?" I laugh, admiring the view of her ass, my sweats stretched tight over the plump cheeks of her backside. "Not even a child would fit through there, little storm."

"Yes, well," she huffs, "You didn't leave me much choice."

"What more do I need to give you, princess?"

"Take me home."

"No."

"Then leave me here to die trapped in this fucking window." She growls out on a defeated sigh, her body slumping awkwardly.

"Not going to do that either."

"I'm stuck." She sighs.

"I can see that." I cock my head, peering beneath her. She had lodged her hips into the window but that wasn't what was keeping her there. No, the sweats are caught on a piece of the frame, all tangled up and the more she moves, the tighter it gets.

"Would you like some help?" I offer.

"Well, obviously, asshole."

My hand smooths up the back of her thigh and she stills.

"Say please."

"Everett!"

"Come on princess, use those manners," I tease, my hand running up and down the back of her leg.

Her body shivers. "Cold?" I ask.

"Please," She grits out.

"Good girl," I praise and revel in her little gasp of shock. "I'm going to need to cut these off."

"What!?"

"They're stuck," I advise, "And it's the easiest way to free you."

"Fine," She snaps, "But can we hurry it up, I'm getting frost bite on my nose."

Laughing, "You'll be fine for another five minutes." I tell her as I leave her hanging from the window and go search for the scissors.

CHAPTER SEVENTEEN
arryn

So, this wasn't my smartest idea. To be fair, I did think I'd be able to shimmy my way through the gap, though I hadn't entirely thought the plan through. My hips wouldn't fit but I would have been able to free myself if I hadn't got the sweats caught on whatever it was beneath me.

And I knew Everett was reveling in this.

His chuckle was still ringing in my head. And I hated that I liked the sound of his laugh. It was so damn hard to stay angry at him. I put on a great show but fuck, the man had more charm than I knew what to do with. I was usually a woman immune to such things, yet here I fucking was, melting a little at the way that chuckle had sent goose bumps chasing down my spine.

I could blame the cold biting at my face, but I knew it wasn't that.

I hated that I reacted to him.

I could pretend all I fucking wanted, but physically there was no denying what he did to me. Even trapped in this damn window I reacted to the feel of his hand on my leg, running so softly up the back of my thigh but he stopped a few inches from my center and then he'd run it back down and done it again. It lasted barely a few seconds, but I could still feel the burn of his touch like it was a brand on my skin.

Cabin fever. It had to be.

I hear him return, his cheery whistle echoing in the bathroom. "Stay still, princess," He tells me, "I don't want to cut your pretty skin."

I hold still as I feel him pull at the cuff at the bottom and then I feel the cold slide of metal as the backside of the scissors moves up my leg. He makes quick work on one side, cutting it all the way up to the waistband before he moves to the other side.

If I wasn't so focused on where his fingers brush the bare skin of my legs, I would be mortified that I was about to be bare assed and sticking out a window.

"Almost there," He whispers.

I focus on the scissors until he cuts the final section, and the material falls away. I wasn't wearing underwear.

"Fuck," I hear him grumble.

I start to move, my cheeks flaming hot despite the cold, but he quickly stops me, "Watch yourself on that metal."

He helps guide me out and once I am free and upright, his sweatshirt falls down over me, stopping around midthigh to cover me back up. He brings my back to his chest as he leans around me to pull the window closed, shutting out the cold.

My eyes fall closed when his lips brush the shell of my ear, "Am I so bad you'd risk the weather to escape me?"

Skilled hands brush the hair away from the side of my face, so much tender in comparison to the way he gripped and pulled it earlier, hard enough that there was a delicious bite of pain on my scalp that had done things to me I didn't know was possible.

It was so strange to be aroused by the sudden lack of control around him, as a woman who liked control on all things, it confused me. Perhaps that was why I was fighting him so hard.

I knew I needed to stay here even if I didn't want to, but the logical side of my brain and the stubborn, combative side were warring. I didn't want to die. The fear and the grief didn't help, putting me in a constant state of agitation.

"I feel trapped." I admit.

The tips of his fingers run up the side of my thigh, stopping at the hem of the sweater.

"Keep talking, princess, what else?" He whispers.

"I'm scared."

He runs his nose up the underside of my ear, "And?"

"I'm incredibly sad." My voice catches on the word.

Where the fuck was this vulnerability coming from? Why was I letting him see this?

I choke it down, swallowing the lump building in my throat. He opens his mouth to talk, and I could already guess what he was going to say but I didn't want to do that, so I spin around.

I needed something else right now. I needed to stop these feelings, stop this sudden wave of emotion and I knew exactly how to shut that shit down.

I lunge for his mouth, his arms barely coming around to catch me as I practically climb the man like a tree. He groans into my mouth, a deep throaty sound that sends a wave of heat through my body. He hoists me up his body and I wrap my legs around his waist, my bare center pressing against him as he turns us and places me down on the bathroom counter, a hand suddenly coming up to grab a fistful of my hair. He yanks my head back, exposing my throat.

His cock presses teasingly against me and I knew I was soaked for him, the burning need to be filled and fucked, overpowering that emotion that had tried to consume me moments ago.

Everett licks his way up my throat, that hand still tangled up in my hair, forcing me to remain in this position for him, leaving him entirely in control with my legs wrapped around his waist, bared for him beneath the oversized sweatshirt that has ridden up to expose me fully. There was no escaping him. No getting out of this hold. And I found I didn't want to. I liked giving him the control, not having to worry about my next move or my next words, knowing he was completely in charge here and I was just coming along for the ride.

"Keep talking, little storm," he rasps against my skin, "What else?"

"Don't," I beg, "I don't want to feel, Everett."

"You don't want to feel, princess?" He chuckles, "Not even this?" His hand works between us and strokes up my inner thigh, a feather light caress that shoots sparks through me.

"Just this," I whimper, groaning when that hand in my hair tightens to the point of pain and my neck stretches further. His tongue licks over the fluttering pulse point in my throat.

"Just this," he repeats, "You want me to consume you so thoroughly all you can feel is me working between these pretty thighs?" His teeth sink into my neck, and I cry out at the sudden pain, my brain unable to comprehend why it felt so fucking good and so bad at the same time. My pussy clenches as he rolls his hard cock against me, my heart hitching up a notch in speed as I become a desperate, needy mess.

"Yes!" I groan.

"Tell me I own this cunt, little storm," He demands hoarsely, consumed by his desire for me. I've been desired before but never like this, like if he didn't get me, he'd never survive.

"You own it," I comply. Fuck my inner feminist at this point. He can have it if it'll stop this fucking ache.

"That's fucking right, princess. I own it." He finally rewards me with a swipe of his hand on my clit, just a delicate circle with the tips of his fingers but it's enough to make me whimper and try to grind against it. "I can make you forget it all for a moment, Arryn, tell me that's what you want."

"It's what I want, Everett, please."

"Good girl," He praises, pressing harder against me, using his fingers to work me up to the peak of a climax but dangling me at the edge. Every time it's right there, he lets it go, never letting me fall off.

"Please!" I beg. "God, I need to come."

"This is how I've felt," He growls, "Balancing on this edge until I thought I was going to go fucking crazy."

"Just – I *need*," I groan at the sudden yank of my hair, halting the words on my tongue.

"I know what you need," He rasps, "You need my cock to fill up this needy pussy until all you can remember is my name as you scream it over and over again."

He suddenly lets my hair go and lifts me off the counter, planting me on my feet before he spins me until I'm facing myself in the mirror.

"Look how beautiful you are, little storm," He drags the hem of the sweater up, capturing the cami underneath at the same time as he pulls them both over my head. I was completely naked for him, nipples peaked and aching, chest heaving, and skin flushed. I looked wild, my hair a mess from his hand, cheeks burning pink with kiss swollen lips. "All of this was made for me," He tells me, "So elegant, princess," his hand runs up my arm and over the curve of my shoulder, "so much grace. And this neck," he lets his whole hand wrap around my throat, the size of it covering me from clavicle to jaw. "You are regal," He declares.

Where his skin was tan, mine was pale in comparison, his hands rough against the softness of me.

"Look at you," He grins behind me, triumphantly, a little menacing but then his teeth sink into his bottom lip as he lets his glacial eyes drop to my breasts and the hand not holding my throat comes up to cup one. He pushes it up as he lets his thumb and forefinger pinch the hardened nipple between them, rolling the sensitive nub between them almost painfully.

I wanted to cry for mercy, but I knew he wasn't prepared to give me it.

"I want you to watch, princess," He growls, "Watch me completely own this body. Watch and see how fighting is pointless between us, you are made for me and only me. Watch while I fuck you and prove to you there is no one else but me."

His hand suddenly comes away from my throat and he grabs my hair once more, wrapping the dark strands around his fist, "Bend forward, Arryn," He orders, "but keep watching."

Shakily, I bend forward, pressing my ass into his hard length which makes his eyes roll back in pleasure. He may control this; I think almost giddily, but I control him too. He was as desperate as I was.

"I'm going to fuck you bare, princess," He tells me, "You're going to take my cock raw and I'm going to fill you up until I'm dripping down these thighs."

No one had ever fucked me bare before. I wasn't worried about pregnancies; I had an implant for birth control, but it was something I felt was too intimate. But I didn't want to stop him, so I let him and watch him as he yanks his sweats down, freeing himself with one hand, the other still tangled in my hair.

He grips his shaft and dips his head, running the head of it through me, finding me more than ready to take him. My eyes close at the sensation of it, the thick head of him parting me, teasing across the sensitive bundle of nerves before he slips it to my entrance, pressing in just an inch, my body stretching to fit him.

A sudden tug on my hair has my eyes snapping open.

"Watch me fuck you, Arryn. Do not take your eyes off the mirror princess or I'll keep you aching for the rest of the day."

CHAPTER EIGHTEEN
everett

I drop my eyes to where the tip of my cock disappears into her tight cunt, her wetness soaking me. Goddamn, she was perfect, her hair wrapped around my fist, graceful neck arched as I pull her head back.

My eyes bounce to the mirror where her eyes are watching my face. I grin at her slackened lips, lids threatening to close at the pleasure I'm pushing into her body. With her eyes latched onto mine I slam into her body, burying myself balls deep, her tightness squeezing me as her body adjusts at the sudden intrusion. She cries out, nails clawing at the bathroom countertop and her eyes flutter closed. I yank her hair and again her eyes snap open, and she glares at me.

"Keep. Watching." I grunt, thrusting into her hard

HURRICANE

enough our bodies slap together and her body jolts forward with every slam of my hips. I ride her from behind hard and fast, fist tangled in her black mane of hair.

Her glare turns heated, and I grab her hip with the hand not holding her hair, using both to pull her onto my cock with each pump of my hips.

"Fuck yes," She cries.

We watch each other, faces twisted in pleasure as I continue to fuck her, listening to her cries like they're music. She takes each hard thrust of my hips, swallows up my cock into her tight little body, but I needed deeper.

I let go of her hair and her head falls forward, but she corrects herself, lifting her chin to watch me beneath her lashes. I reach down and grasp one thigh, forcing her leg up so her knee is resting on the edge of the counter, and straighten her spine, holding her to me by one hand at her throat. I adjust and slam up into her, watching her watch me in the mirror, my hand cupping her jaw, the other holding her open for me and I punish her with hard, fast thrusts.

"God, keep going," She mewls, "Don't stop, Everett. Please."

"That's it, princess," I praise, "Look how good we fit together," I say, "So fucking beautiful."

She is damn pretty like this, all of her body on show for me, that pretty cunt dripping for me, soaking my cock and thighs as I fuck her hard. She takes it so damn well.

"Play with your pretty pussy, little storm," I order, "Get yourself off on my cock. I want you to come all over me."

She immediately drops a hand to herself, rolling the tips of her fingers against her needy little cunt.

"Part yourself," I tell her, "Let me see how you fuck yourself Arryn."

She groans, head dropping back onto my shoulder, but she keeps her eyes open and on us. I watch in the reflection as she parts her lips and scissors her fingers through her folds, teasing herself before she pays attention to the swollen nub at the top of her dripping slit.

"Everett," She moans my name, "I'm going to come."

"That's right," I thrust, feeling her inner walls beginning to flutter as her climax barrels to the surface. "Give it to me."

Her cunt squeezes me like a vice as she cries out with her orgasm. "Fuuuccckkkkk!" I groan, my hips losing rhythm as my climax whips down my spine. I thrust hard, once, twice, three times before I lose myself inside of her, emptying myself with a long moan.

She leans forward, resting her elbows on the counter as I lean across her back, my lips at the nape of her neck. Her breathing is hard and fast, skin slickened with sweat. Standing, I look down as I slip from her body, using my hands to part her, watching as I leak from her.

"So damn perfect," I murmur, using a single finger to

swipe up my come and push it back inside her, fucking her with my finger. She moans needily, pushing back on my hand for more.

"What a greedy little thing you are," I muse, "You want more, princess?"

"Mm," She hums, pressing back on the finger. I add a second, letting her use my hand to find her second release. A mix of her and me soaks my hand, and I add a third finger, stretching her open.

"God," she whimpers.

"He isn't here right now, little storm, just me. So, if you're going to worship anyone, worship me."

I help her pace, pumping my fingers with every roll of her own hips, pushing my fingers into her. "What do you want?" I ask her.

"You," She whimpers, "More, please."

"Sit your ass on the counter," I order, helping her wobbly legs to turn and aid her into sitting on the side. I drop to my knees between her legs, fingers still buried inside of her body, pumping and thrusting into her and then I lean in and suck her swollen clit into my mouth, flicking my tongue against her and feeling her hips grind into my face.

"Shit!" She moans loudly, hand latching onto my hair to hold me to her. I keep up with my pace, her hand tightening in my hair until she detonates. Her pussy flutters on my tongue but I keep thrusting my hand, prolonging the orgasm until she's physically pushing me away from the over stimulation.

She slumps back, her spine resting on the mirror as hooded eyes follow me while I gather some cloths to clean her up.

I swipe between her legs, grinning when she flinches as I wipe over her pussy. "Get in the shower, princess. I'll make you food."

"Unicorn." She mutters. "A crazy one though."

"Sorry?"

"You're a unicorn."

"I'm not following, princess," I pull up my sweats, cocking my head as she picks up a towel to cover herself.

"You know, a fictional creature."

"I can assure you I am very real, or do I need to prove it again?"

"Well first, you make me come hard during sex and that just doesn't happen, then you do it again with your mouth and you didn't even care that your come was still dripping out of me, and now you're going to make me food? This shit only happens in books. Men just don't do this. It makes it almost possible to forgive the whole kidnapping shit."

I step up to her, lifting a hand to swipe across her plump bottom lip. Her eyes drop to my mouth, ready for me to kiss her but I don't.

"I'll correct something for you, little storm. *Men* do this. They worship their women, get pleasure through watching them fall apart, they feed them and take care of them because that's what they want to do. Don't confuse me with the *boys* you've been with before. They don't matter. There is only me. And you are mine."

Her eyes widen and then I kiss her, letting her taste us on her tongue.

"And I didn't kidnap you," I yank at the towel, forcing it from her, "It's called relocation."

"Kidnap," she snaps back. "And you drugged me, let's not forget that."

"Well, you would have screamed the whole town down," I defend, "Get in the shower."

I don't wait for whatever retort she's ready to throw back at me. I leave her to clean up and head into the kitchen, washing my hands before I start to prepare the dinner from whatever ingredients we have left. This snow needed to stop soon otherwise we would run out.

I have the dinner cooking when Arryn comes out, wet hair pulled across one shoulder as she dries it with a towel. "That smells amazing. Who taught you to cook?"

"I did, princess."

"Your mom?"

"Didn't know her. I left home early," I turn my back on her as she takes a seat at the table, curiosity stamped on her face, "Had to figure it out pretty quick if I didn't want to survive on ramen and eggs for the rest of my life."

"And you learnt that in between killing people?"

Curiosity… it was a bitch, wasn't it?

"Yeah princess."

"You know, I believed there were people like you, I'm not naïve enough to believe hitmen or assassins don't exist, but I never expected to meet one."

"We're a necessity," I tell her, pulling plates from the cupboard.

"How do you figure that, Everett?" She asks.

"Because without us there would be no one to cull the greedy and corrupt."

"There are still greedy and corrupt people."

"There always will be but now there are a little less."

"But that's not the only people you accept jobs for, is it? My father," Her voice chokes on that, "The Wares were just competition."

"I was raised to do this, Arryn, I don't care much who I am targeting. Just that I am getting paid for it. And the Ware's aren't exactly clean now, are they?"

"No," She agrees.

I place a plate of food in front of her, handing her a glass of whiskey and a fork, "You don't have to be scared of me, princess."

She takes them both, "I'm not scared of you, Everett."
Her eyes meet mine, "I pity you."

CHAPTER NINETEEN
arryn

You know what they don't teach you in school?

How to braid your own hair.

This shit is a whole arm work out and puzzle all at the same time. This piece wraps over this one, and this one under that one, all the while your arms are going dead from being upright too long. And don't get me started when it isn't tight enough or you miss a strand and have to do it all over.

Like I just did.

I stifle a frustrated scream and rip the braid loose. My sister used to braid my hair and I used to do hers after our mother died but it was our mom who taught us. She used to braid it for us all the time, even as we got older, she used to do it. Mine and then Olivia's.

I hang my head, pushing back memories.

God this silence was really playing tricks, clearly. It was so silent here you could hear the snow falling outside.

"Here," Everett says.

My head snaps up to him. He's holding the comb and sitting with his knees parted, a pillow already between his feet ready for me to sit.

"What?"

"Come here."

Curious, I shuffle over to him, sitting between his knees. He immediately starts combing my hair, bringing it away from my face and sectioning it gently. And then he begins to… braid it.

He does it quietly, gently, simply braiding my hair like he's done it his whole life.

"How?"

"I have a niece," He murmurs quietly, "I wanted to learn for her."

"How old is she?"

"Nine now," He says, "I only met her last year. Her name is Harper. She's sweet, been through a lot in her short life and the men from before failed her."

"Before?"

"She isn't my brother's daughter, but she may as well

be. Maya, my sister-in-law, she came from a bad place with her daughter and then she met Torin, that's my brother, and I wanted it to be my job to show that little girl not all men are like her dad."

"What happened?"

"Not my story to tell," He says, "But I learned how to braid hair so I could do hers. Her mother does it for her, but I wanted to learn too. Torin and I watched videos," He laughs quietly, "Even went out and got one of those mannequins that salons use for practice."

"Torin learned how, too?"

"Yeah," He replies.

"That's actually really sweet," My breath catches.

He ties the band to secure the braid and smooths his hand over the ridges of the style, tugging playfully on the end.

Being around Everett Avery was kind of like getting whiplash. It wasn't hot and cold; it was kind and gentle to crazy and unhinged. The lines between the two versions were becoming incredibly blurred.

"You said you pity me," Everett says, bringing me from my thoughts, "What is it you pity?"

I turn between his legs and cross my own, watching as he leans back on the couch, his knees spread as I continue to sit between them.

"That instead of enjoying life, you steal it instead."

One side of his mouth cocks up into a semblance of a smirk, "And you?"

"What about me?"

"Do you pity yourself?"

"Why would I do that?"

"Because you may not steal life, but do you enjoy it?"

"I have – *had,*" I correct, "a wonderful life."

He quirks a brow in disbelief, "Tell me something good then."

"About my life?"

Slowly, he leans forward, and I force myself to remain still. Nerves flitter through my body at his proximity, the way my body reacts to him, despite the circumstances, is something that still confuses me.

His finger curls beneath my chin, "Yes, little storm, something good in your life. Something you truly enjoy that no one else knows."

His eyes bounce around my face as if committing every one of my features to memory. He looks at me like I'm something to worship.

"Sundays." I breathe.

"Sundays," He repeats.

"They are sacred." I tell him, "A day for me. A day for me to do whatever I want. Read a book. Have a glass of wine. Walk in the park."

"Why Sundays to do these things?" He enquires, genuinely curious.

"Because Monday through Saturday I belong to everyone else. Magazines, my father, the hotel."

"And your lingerie boutique?"

"That doesn't feel like a job," I sigh, "I enjoy creating and distributing for every type of woman. I don't do it for the partners. We as a society assume women wearing lingerie is for someone else, for husbands and boyfriends, for girlfriends and wives but I wanted to create something that made people feel good, for them and them only. It is my brand. To create something for the body to make *you* feel good and not anyone else. If someone chooses to share it with their partner then fine, but when I wear lingerie, I do it for myself. I don't much care if another person sees it."

"So not just Sundays."

"I guess not just Sundays, but I don't have enough time for it anymore." I admit.

"What books do you read?" He changes the subject but the look on his face suggests it's not a topic we will be forgetting.

My cheeks heat, "I like romance."

Everett smiles wide, "Yeah? What kind of romance, princess?"

"All of them. I just like the burn it all to the ground for her kind of romance. When nothing and no one compares." My voice takes on a wistful kind of lilt.

"It's a type of love that doesn't exist outside of books, no one is that devoted."

"Is that your expert opinion?"

"It's fact," I shrug, "I've never once seen the type of love in the books I read."

"So, because you haven't seen it, it doesn't exist?"

I open my mouth to defend myself but then I have nothing to say about that. Just because I hadn't seen it, witnessed it, doesn't mean it doesn't exist.

"I think because you haven't experienced it," Everett continues, his thumb stroking softly across my jaw, "You believe it's not possible. But I've witnessed the all-consuming, heart shattering love you're talking about. I've seen what it can do and what it can cause, and I assure you, princess, it's real."

"And you want it?" I ask.

"I'm working on it," He smiles, leaning in closer, closing the space between us until his lips are almost touching mine. I feel the warmth of his breath on my lips and stare into the glacial blue of his eyes. This close I can see the specks of darker blue freckled throughout, some lighter parts that look like lightning forked through the blue of his iris's.

I could imagine being loved by a man like Everett would be intense and a longing kind of feeling blooms in my chest. The feeling makes me realize just how lonely my life has been, how walled off I've made myself.

Then I'm kicking myself because this is a man who kills for a living.

And I'm just the woman he's currently taken a shining to. It would never last.

The two of us, with all these differences…we were just messy.

CHAPTER TWENTY
arryn

"You don't have to sleep there," I hover at the mouth of the hallway that leads to the one bedroom in this cabin, chewing on my bottom lip. Everett glances over to me from where he's sprawled across the couch, the blanket resting at his hips and his bare, sculptured chest on show, the dark ink etched into his skin drawing my eyes as the firelight kisses his skin. He has one hand resting behind his head, stretching out those thick arm muscles.

He is a beautiful man, every hard, glorious inch of him.

I never stood a fucking chance.

"You want me to sleep with you, princess?" He smirks, catching me ogling him like a damn piece of meat. It was hardly fair for him to look like that. Like I said, he was a unicorn. He may as well have walked right off a romance book page because he was living up to every book boyfriend dream.

"No," I instantly defend, crossing my arms, "I just don't see much point in you sleeping out here. It can't be comfortable."

"Will you try to murder me in my sleep?" He teases, sitting up. His back is just as pretty as the front, broad shoulders, muscles that ripple and flex when he moves but littered with scars. There was a new one on his shoulder, fresh and pink, still raised, which oddly looked like a bullet wound.

I avert my eyes and start walking towards the bedroom, "I make no promises."

His chuckle follows me through the door, making my damn knees weak and raising goose bumps over my skin.

"Stupid, stupid girl," I mutter to myself, throwing back the sheets to climb into the bed. The lamp on the bedside counter gives the room a warm glow and I'd purposely left the curtains open to see the still falling snow outside the window.

There was so much snow, piled so high outside the windows it almost touched the glass. Everett had been shoveling every day, several times a day just to keep it clear but this was just ridiculous. How could one place get so much snow?

But there was no denying the peace that came with the small white flakes falling from the sky, I'd always thought it back in the city when I actually had time to enjoy it, rather than battling it.

Laying with the sheets still pulled back, Everett strolls through the bedroom door a moment later, a pair of sweats hanging low on his hips. A trail of hair works from his naval to beneath his pants, framed by that delicious V that carves up his hips and will make any woman lose a few brain cells. What is it about an Adonis belt that makes us go crazy?

"The way you look at me, little storm, makes me want to do real bad things to you." Everett rasps, taking easy, controlled steps towards me on the bed. I curl my fingers into the sheets, holding my breath while he places a knee onto the end of the mattress and then the other until he's kneeling at my feet and staring at me like he wants to eat me.

The hunger that burns in his gaze is enough to set my whole body on fire and warmth spreads through me, the man hasn't even touched me.

There was no room for any other thought, any worries or grief or anger, just him and me and the inferno of undeniable chemistry that flares between us.

He places his hand on one of my ankles, circling his fingers around it before he does the same on the other, tightening his grip and then he yanks me down the bed, moving me so effortlessly towards him. I yelp before his body covers mine and his lips land against my own. Helpless is how I felt and yet a big part of me did not want to be saved from him.

He breathes me in like I'm the very air that fills his lungs. No man had ever consumed me the way Everett does, and it had only been a few days.

The fire will dwindle, surely, it couldn't remain this...*intense.*

His tongue tangles with mine, hands coming up to frame my head so he can angle it just the way he wants. He dominates me, controls every aspect of this and I can't help but submit to it, let him have it. I don't want control here, not when I have to control every other aspect of my life. Right here, right now, with him, I want him to have it. I don't want to make the choices, the decisions, I just want to feel this.

"The way you melt for me," He growls against my mouth, his fingers threading into my hair right before he grips the strands and tugs slightly, bringing my head back, chin up while he stares down at me, "I love how you trust me with your body. You know I can make you feel good."

"Yes," I whisper, unable to deny it.

From that first night to now, despite everything in between, I've always known he'd treat my body like it was a temple.

"We are inevitable, princess," He captures my bottom lip in his teeth, adding a bite of pain right before he rolls his hard cock up between my legs, "Just like the devastation that comes after a hurricane, there is no stopping us."

"It's only for now," my sentence ends on a moan as he grinds into me.

He chuckles, "No, no princess," hands come away from my hair and down my body where he yanks up the cami and cups the undersides of my breasts. "You're mine. I don't share. I don't give in. When you're mine, you are *mine*. I am keeping you."

He moves down my body to press kisses against my stomach, making my muscles jump and twitch at the contact of his lips to my skin. "I will keep you safe, and happy. Worship you. Care for you. Destroy anyone who dares to hurt you."

His declaration startles me and I sit up, ready to make him stop. No, this was too much. He was too much. But then his teeth capture a nipple, and he bites, the sting of it enough to make me yelp but then his tongue soothes the hurt and his hand gently presses me back down.

"There's no use fighting me, Arryn, you were made for me. I hadn't realized I was waiting for you until I met you and now, you're here, with me, under me, on my tongue, under my hands, buried so far into my skin there will be no getting you out."

"Everett, stop," My hand slides into his hair, gripping the thick, dark strands to keep his mouth against my breast.

I feel him grin against me and then he moves his attention to the other breast, the sensation of it rushing tingles down my spine until my thighs ache with the need for him.

"Stop what, princess?" He flicks his eyes up to me, looking at me from beneath his lashes, "You want me to stop worshipping you?" A hand slips beneath the waist of my pants and finds my soaked center, his fingers sliding through me so easily I should be embarrassed at how wet I am for the man.

"No, don't stop," I beg, "Just shut up."

"So bossy," He teases, "but here in the bedroom, you are not in control."

"It's too much for you to keep saying those things," I groan as a finger dips inside, my spine arching away from the mattress.

"The truth scares you," He kisses me, "but with you, I cannot lie."

"You don't know me, Everett," My eyes latch onto his, "This is lust talking."

"I know enough," he adds a second finger, "Enough to know that there is no one better suited for you, than me."

"Oh god," I cry out as he presses his thumb to my clit and pumps his fingers purposely slow.

"You don't love me right now, little storm, but you will." He promises.

"Everett," I plead.

"Come for me," He whispers, kissing across my jaw, working me with his hand until stars burst behind my eyes and I clench around the fingers buried inside of me. "That's it," He rasps, "so fucking beautiful when you fall apart."

He works me until the orgasm dims and I'm a mess on the bed, limbs heavy and chest heaving, body still shaking as I come down.

He withdraws his hand, his body still propped over mine and then he brings that hand up and sucks the fingers that were inside me into his mouth, groaning as if the taste of me is the best thing that's ever touched his tongue.

And then he rolls off me and drags the sheets over us, not bothering to try turn the light off which I assumed he would, and I'd have to explain why.

But he doesn't ask, instead choosing to pull me closer to him, holding me in the cradle of his arms.

"Don't you…" I trail off, hoping he understands what I'm trying to say. But he doesn't respond so I move my hand down between us, ready to give back what he'd given me, but he captures my wrist.

"Go to sleep, princess," He murmurs.

"But…" I could feel how hard he was, he had to be aching.

"I just want to hold you." He tells me. "Just let me hold you."

CHAPTER TWENTY-ONE

everett

I wake the following morning sweating my ass off. Arryn's mane of thick black hair is thrown over my face, one leg and arm clinging to my body as her head rests on my shoulder. My fingers flex on her waist where I hold her to me, some deeper part of me easing at the way her body feels so perfect with mine. She breathes deeply and evenly, still sleeping soundly.

But I had some work to do this morning, and needed to get up to get it done before she wakes.

Carefully detangling myself from her, I tuck her back in and shower before I dress and head outside. The snow had finally stopped, the sky a clear blue this morning though the sun had some work to do to get rid of all this snow on the ground. I shovel around the cabin, clearing it away before I head back in and make coffee, setting myself up at the table to log in to the computer.

The message pops up as soon as it loads.

Everything is ready for you. The cameras are installed in three places, here is the link to access them. We will be on site as requested.

Perfect.

I'd had to pull some favors to get this done and since I couldn't be on the mainland to do it, this was the best I could come up with.

It wouldn't be exactly what she needs but it's the best I can give her right now.

I had a couple of hours to go before it started so I do my daily check and search for the Ware's, coming up empty once again and check the hit on Arryn. A new man had been assigned to the job since the last had failed to find her.

I had people searching for the Ware's, but no one was coming up with any information, and there was a limit to what I could do from this cabin without all of my equipment. They were big names in society, how do they just disappear?

What exactly were they involved in and how the fuck did I miss it?

I call Torin who confirms the forecast is clear for the next few days, giving the cabin, and the tiny little town at the foot of the cliff a reprieve from the icy storm. He said he'd be heading to the mainland to grab supplies.

I couldn't risk him going to Arryn's house to gather her some belongings since anyone could be watching, and waiting, and all it would take would be someone following Torin back. He could handle himself, but it wasn't a risk I was willing to take. It would jeopardize the safety this town and this cabin provided. But he could go shopping for her.

"I'm not clothes shopping for your girlfriend, Rett," He grunts down the line.

"Just a few things," I say, "Nothing fancy. Take Maya, I'm sure she wouldn't mind."

"And how am I supposed to explain to Maya why I'm buying women's clothes?"

"Shit." I grunt.

"Yeah, shit."

"Torin, just some items, the girl has been living in my sweats and tees for days."

"I really hate you." Torin growls.

"Love you too brother," I laugh, "I'll try get down into town to grab them."

"Don't break your neck on that cliffside, Everett. No one will find you."

"Charming." I shake my head, "Speak soon."

Torin hangs up without a goodbye, the grumpy fuck, and I lay the phone down on the table just as Arryn makes an appearance from the bedroom.

She's still dozy, her hair mused and a yawn stretching her mouth open, "Who was you speaking to?" She asks sleepily, trudging towards the chair in front of me.

I get up to make her some coffee, "My brother."

"He knows?"

"About?"

"Everything?"

"Yes," I tell her, "We were all raised the same. He knows you're here and why. He can be trusted."

"This is the same one you were telling me about?" She asks curiously, "The one who married that girl with the kid?"

"Her name is Maya, Harper is her daughter, yes. You'll like them."

She doesn't look convinced, "Not many people like me, Everett."

I pause, "What?"

"I'm a convenience," She shrugs, accepting the coffee with a small smile, "Always have been. My family like me, of course, and Suzy, she was my assistant. But I don't have friends, just acquaintances. Most people only put up with me because they had something to gain."

I'm stumped, then I'm fucking furious "No one will ever use you again, princess. I won't allow it."

But she just sighs, "It's okay, really. You get used to being alone." She glances towards the windows, "Hey, it stopped snowing."

"Come here," I call to Arryn a few hours later. She pads over to me, hair pulled across one shoulder as it dries from her shower.

"What is it?"

"I didn't want you to miss it," I tell her quietly, a pang of guilt tightening my stomach, "But I couldn't risk taking you."

"What are you talking about?"

I turn the screen her way, showing her the live feed of her father's service.

She sucks in a breath, agony twisting her face as grief makes her eyes well with tears.

"Why did you do this?" Her voice cracks on a sob and I move in, pulling her to me and situating her on my lap.

"Because I didn't want you to miss it, princess, this is the best I could do. I am so sorry."

Her eyes are glued to the screen as people start to make their way inside the building ready for Victor's service to begin.

"How?" Her hand curls around my arm as if being on my lap isn't enough physical connection and she needs more. I hold her tighter.

"I have friends," Is all I tell her.

"My sister," She gasps, leaning in further as if she could climb through it and stand right by her sister's side. Olivia Lauder is beautiful, very similar to Arryn in looks but where Arryn had blue eyes, Olivia had such dark eyes they almost looked black. Shorter hair which was wavy over the dead straight of Arryn's.

Suzy, Arryn's assistant stands with Olivia and a second woman who I didn't know stands at her other side. They both support the young girl, tears tracking down her face and smearing her fresh makeup.

"I should be there." Arryn whispers sadly, "I should be holding her."

"I know, princess," Arryn furiously swipes at her tears.

"How can you be sure it wouldn't be safe?" She asks.

I lean in next to her and point to the screen, "These two people here," I point to two men that look like security, "Are men I hired to keep watch on the service. I want to know if the Ware's show up, but I also wanted them there to protect your sister in case something was to happen." She nods, following my hand as I move it across the screen to a third man. I knew him, even had drinks with the man once upon a time. He was a well sought after hitman, almost as sought after as Torin, me, and Kolt, and I *knew* he was the man who had taken the job over. "This man right here works in the organization. He's a very skilled assassin, I didn't hire him for the service, and I very much doubt he's there to pay his respects. He's waiting to see if you show up."

"He'd just murder me in front of all these people?"

"No, little storm," I keep my eye on him, watching as he stalks every attendee, watches them all like a hawk, reading their faces, waiting for my Arryn to arrive. "He'd stalk you, mark you and when you're alone, he'd strike. Once he has his eyes on you, he won't lose you. Even if I was with you."

"Oh my god, is Olivia safe?"

"She hasn't got a hit out on her," I tell her, "It's just you. I don't think the Ware's intended to involve Victor's daughters, you just happened to witness them killing two men and therefore you're a liability."

"But if they killed my dad because he's the competition, then why would he not take us out? Since we're the ones to take over the hotel and remain the competition."

"I'm not sure, Arryn, I have people looking into them but they're very good at hiding their tracks."

"Fucking assholes," Arryn grumbles, "I hate them. Are you sure my sister is safe?"

"Those men there are watching her," I assure her, "Day and night. She is guarded."

"Thank you," She breathes, "I just don't understand how we all got in this mess."

"Unfortunately," I kiss away a lone tear, "darkness and death have always ruled, it's just hard to see."

She watches her father's service in silence. She keeps track of her younger sister, sobbing quietly on my lap while she makes her speech. She addresses the room, pleading for information again on Arryn's whereabouts before they're all silenced in preparation for Victor's burial.

The hitman targeting Arryn never leaves. He remains a stoic presence at the back of the room, the guys I have employed standing close to him. I could order a hit on him, but it wouldn't do much good, someone else would only take over the job.

Arryn got one thing right, this whole situation was a mess, and it was getting impossible to clean.

CHAPTER TWENTY-TWO

everett

Arryn didn't speak a single word after the service ended. She sat bundled under blankets in front of the fire. But she didn't cry again. Her eyes were rimmed red, her skin pale and almost sickly and I didn't know what the fuck to do to help her.

I place a new mug by her side and take away the one from before, still full but long gone cold. Her vacant eyes pass over the mug once before she goes back to staring at the fire.

I had to believe letting her see her father lain to rest was the best thing to do but now I'm wondering how much damage I have done.

Or was this simply how grief worked? I didn't know, I've only dealt with three deaths in my life. My father trained these kinds of emotions out of us, or he tried to at least. It didn't work so much on my brother Torin; Kolten was just a bottomless pit anyway and I was somewhere in the middle.

I didn't know what to do.

"You need to drink something, princess."

"I'm okay," She murmurs, facing the flames. The glow of the fire dances across her face, highlighting the deep shadows under her eyes, the dried tear tracks on her cheeks. Her eyes were blank, nothing warm or lively was in that stare.

"Princess," I plead, getting to my knees at her side.

Slowly, she turns her face towards me and lets her eyes drop down my frame. Not in any other way than bored before she leans in and kisses me. It shocks me enough that for a minute I just let her before my mind kicks back into play.

I pull away from her, but she follows, "Stop." I order.

"Just kiss me," she whispers, climbing on my lap and straddling my thighs.

"No, stop, Arryn."

And now I understood. She didn't like these feelings; this intensity of her sorrow was eating at her, and she was prepared to use me here and now to get rid of those feelings. While I have no problems letting her use me whichever way she pleased, I wasn't going to allow her to bury these feelings like I was taught to do.

I do not believe the way I handle emotion is healthy and I'll be damned if I let this woman drown in darkness. It changes people. And Arryn was perfect the way she was.

"I let you push your feelings away once, little storm, not this time. You need to feel them."

"No, it hurts," She whimpers, attempting to kiss me again. I grip her chin, stopping her, seeing fresh tears fill her eyes, turning the color almost neon against the darkness of her lashes and hair.

"I know it hurts, princess, but the pain tells you how much it means. You lost your dad, and I haven't seen you grieve him. You need to grieve him, baby, otherwise you'll do so much damage to yourself."

"He wouldn't want me to cry."

"Bullshit." I growl.

"I'm fine. I'm okay." She tries to tell me even as her voice wobbles and tears roll over her cheeks, catching in the corners of her mouth.

"Don't you lie to me, princess." I wipe at her face, catching her sadness on my fingers, "Cry, baby. I've got you."

She shakes her head furiously, "No."

"It's okay," I soothe, "You're okay."

A violent sob heaves from her chest and with it the strength to fight it leaves her. She collapses down onto my chest, her fingers clawing into my shirt to hold me to her. I run my hand down her spine, feeling her body tremble against me, her tears soaking through the material of my shirt.

"I lost them both the same way," she cries, "They both died the same way."

My brows draw down, "Who did?"

"My parents." She whispers.

"What do you mean?" I ask.

"My mother was murdered," She sniffs, hiccupping, "she was murdered in a home invasion. I found her."

"Shit."

"It was so brutal," She whispers, "There was so much blood."

I open my mouth, ready to tell her she didn't need to tell me, that she didn't need to relive it but she's talking before I can, "It was dark, and we'd gone out, but my mom had stayed at home so when we returned, I didn't want to turn on the lights and disturb her."

"Princess…"

"I slipped on her blood," she says in a voice edged in so much pain I wondered how she hadn't shattered before this, "Landed right by her. By the time we got home it was too late, she had bled out. And I was covered in her blood. When it's dark, it's all I can see, all I can feel is her blood on my skin, the feel of it on my palms."

It explained the use of a nightlight, I think to myself.

"And now my dad, I saw him get shot, the bullet, it just went through him like he was made of nothing. And his blood, it went in my mouth." With those words, huge soul trembling sobs crack from her chest, "And now he's really gone. He's never coming back. And I didn't say goodbye."

"It's okay," I soothe, holding her through the pain, keeping my arms bound so tightly around her it's as if I am trying to keep all her pieces together. So much pain trapped inside of her, and she's never let herself feel it.

"I couldn't stop after my mom died, I had to continue so my sister could continue, so my dad could continue. If I stopped and they saw, they would break too. I had to be strong. To do what I needed to do. For the family.

"But I am so tired, Everett. I am so tired of keeping everything under control. Of being this shell of a person to everyone on the outside. I am so afraid of being nothing I give everyone nothing so they can't use me or hurt me. I don't want to be good or in control anymore. I want to live. And breathe. Fuck, I just want to breathe. And have fun. And I can't. I can't."

"I've got you, Arryn," I promise her, "Breathe for me, princess."

She cries harder, clinging to me, "I don't want to be known as the icy bitch who owns a bunch of hotels and dies alone, Everett but now I can't even change it. Because if I go back there, I will die. And who will turn up at my funeral?"

Her limbs tremble violently, and she pulls away from me, remaining on my lap as she grips my shoulders and stares at my face, "The only people who will care if something happened to me are Suzy and Olivia. The rest will either celebrate that I'm dead or spit on my grave because I wronged them in some way. I'll have old dates show up and laugh because they always knew I'd die alone since I wasn't easy and opened my legs for them, or hung off their arm like they were my moon and stars. I'll have people I worked with show up and say, she really should have smiled more, lived a little. There is nothing of me to remember except staged photos and a hotel I don't even want!"

"Breathe," I command, "Goddamn it, woman, *breathe!*"

She sucks in a harsh breath of air, coughing a little since she's just worked herself up to the point, she wasn't actually fucking breathing.

"Jesus Christ, little storm, you are holding all this inside of you," I smooth her tangled hair, "when the world should see your passion."

"You call me a little storm," She whispers, "Yet I'm nothing but a little bit of rain."

"Oh, that isn't true," I wipe the tears on her face even though they continue to fall, "you have the power to devastate, Arryn, in every good way possible. The men before, they were nothing but boys who couldn't handle this. The people who used you, mere blips on your radar because you are so much better than they ever were. And this isn't it for you, Arryn," I vow, "I will stop at nothing to get you the fucking life you deserve."

She slumps on my chest, sniffling, "I hate crying."

"You have a heart, Arryn, you just have to let it out of its cage."

Her hand slips up the ridges of my abdomen to come to a stop over mine, "So do you, Everett. Bigger than you let people believe."

"Is that so, princess?"

"You act like a playboy," she pushes away from me and stands, "But deep down you want what everyone wants."

"What?"

"A happily ever after."

CHAPTER TWENTY-THREE

everett

I couldn't keep this woman trapped here.

She needed to experience life and I needed to give her that.

She lays in my arms; a few hours have passed since that moment in front of the fire and all I can think about is how she has yet to experience any real joy in life. Everything for her is set, planned, thought of before rather than spontaneous and fun.

Granted, I lived a different life to her, did morally questionable things daily, but I like my life.

And I was determined to make Arryn like hers.

There was only so much I could do right now for her,

but this tiny little town, set in the middle of the ocean, was a great way to start.

The following morning the sun beams through the window, the snow staying away for another night. While the ground was still covered in the white stuff, deeper than my knees, we could make it down the cliffside, I was certain of it.

Arryn lays with her back to me, dark, glossy hair spread out behind her. I lift a hand and pluck a strand between my fingers, feeling the silky length against the rough pads of my fingertips. So much perfection wrapped up in my fist.

I roll towards her, lining my body up against the back of hers, burying my face into her hair. She lets out a sigh, pressing her ass back into my hips.

"Wake up, princess," I murmur.

She groans and buries her face into the pillow, wiggling against me.

"Ah ah," I chuckle, kissing her neck, "Time to wake up."

"No." She grunts.

I slide a hand over her waist, dipping it down to the waistband of her – my – sweats. "Wake up."

She arches her spine as I slip the hand beneath the band, finding her bare and warm and inviting. I slip a finger through her folds, eliciting a deep, sleepy moan from her. "My princess doesn't want to wake but she wants to feel good?"

"Mm," She hums.

I add a second finger and begin a sensual stroke against her clit, teasing the tight little bud in small circles until I have her dripping against my hand.

"Fuck, so damn wet for me, little storm," I praise.

"God yes," She whimpers, pressing her ass back into me.

"Pull them down," I order gently.

She wiggles until her sweats are around her knees and I yank my boxers down, bringing out my hard cock. Gripping the back of her neck, I force her further forward, giving me more access to her before I grip one thigh and push it up as much as the sweats will allow.

"I could lose myself in your body, princess," I tell her, lining my cock up to her entrance, "Your cunt is like fucking heaven."

She pushes back, wanting me as much as I am wanting her, and I don't leave her waiting. I thrust forward, sheathing myself into her with a deep satisfied groan, her warmth enveloping me. She cries out at my intrusion, stretching to fit me but I don't stop. I keep one leg up and fuck her hard, rattling our bodies with each, hard, deep thrust.

"Yes, Everett, don't stop," She whimpers, nails clawing at the sheets. I hadn't planned on this this morning, but damn it if I was complaining.

In a quick move, I force her onto her stomach, straddling her thighs and lifting her hips up. I keep sliding in and out of her. She feels so good, so fucking perfect.

I fuck into her from behind, keeping her pinned beneath me as I find pleasure in her body, listening to her moans and feeling her writhe. I slip a hand under her, sliding my fingers through her pussy, finding her drenched for me. She gasps as I circle her clit and begin to play, working her body like it's an instrument I've mastered.

"Everett!" She cries. "*Rett!*"

"Say it again."

"Rett!"

"Fuck!" I grunt, pleasure zapping down my spine. "Come for me, princess. Give it to me."

"Yes," She moans.

I work her harder, thrust harder until I can feel her begin to quiver around me and that simple sensation is enough to send me over the edge. She comes hard on my cock, and I spill myself into her, filling her up to the sound of her cries.

Collapsing down across her back, I inhale her scent and kiss the salt from her skin.

"Time to get up, little storm. I have something I want us to do today."

"You expect me to walk after that?" She laughs, the sound so damn beautiful she may as well have just stopped my heart.

I run my hand over her bare skin, soaking in the glory of her, "Get dressed baby, it's time for you to start living."

I bundle Arryn in layers, adding extra sweatshirts over the ones she already has on and then grab the old waterproofs I found in storage. "You know, layers aren't great in the cold right?" she says, staring at me curiously.

"Shh." I tell her, zipping up the coat that I hoped wasn't so old it was no longer waterproof.

She rolls her eyes, "What are we doing?"

"Going for a little walk," I give some information but not all. I didn't know how she was going to take it, so I didn't want to scare her before providing the whole truth.

"Everett," She admonishes.

"Rett," I correct. "You said it already, you can't take it back."

"Why does it matter so much if I call you Rett?" Arryn questions as I guide her towards the door. The snow was still sticking to the ground, but the skies were a beautiful clear blue, the sun working its hardest to melt it.

"Because Everett is the name I use on jobs, princess," I tell her honestly, "And Rett is used for the people I call family."

She freezes in the doorway, "Oh."

"Come," I coax, "We want to get out as early as we can, the light only sticks for a little while."

She remains quiet as I guide her out of the door and it's ten minutes before she speaks again. "You're not afraid I'll run?"

"A day ago?" I answer, "Maybe. But now, no. I think you now understand the situation a little better."

She nods and accepts my hand as I help her down a few craggy and sharp rocks. It was freezing, our breaths coming out in misty clouds of white and the forest around us was silent. Our feet crunch into the snow and twigs and branches snap on our decline, but an hour into the hike down I start to see the first glimpses of civilization. The town is still a small blip in my vision, but it is visible through the breaks in the trees.

"You see here?" I stop Arryn, pointing towards where the town is a mash of reds and blues and yellows, the store signs and colorful buildings creating a painting against the white and green backdrop.

"What is that?"

"This is Ravenpeak Bay," I tell her proudly.

"I've never heard of it," She breathes, seemingly frozen staring at the blur of the quaint little town. It made me excited to show her the whole of it up close. I can bitch and moan that the town was sleepy and old but there was no place I'd ever called home. Ravenpeak Bay was *home*.

"Not surprising," I say, helping her down this final stretch, "Ravenpeak is one of those towns where you can simply disappear."

We walk the final hour through the trees and steep declines, dodging the rocks and trunks that jut up from the earth, until our feet hit the ground of the lot at the bottom of the trail we followed. It's still covered in snow here, but it's less treacherous.

The walk to Torin's house from here is less than twenty minutes but it didn't pass through the town itself since my brother's house was right on the docks and looked out over the bay.

I take Arryn's hand, suppressing the grin I feel when she links her fingers with mine.

"It's so quiet," She muses.

"Ravenpeak sees tourists through Spring and Summer and a little into Fall, but it remains quiet here regardless. It's peaceful."

"It is," She agrees, taking in the scenery around her. The towering pines, our watchful guards, the tranquil sound of waves crashing on the shore, the music that guides us.

"I've been in cities my whole life," Arryn tells me, "Small towns never even appealed to me until right now."

"This town is different," I explain, "It's just one of those places."

"A story book," She breathes dreamily.

"I'll take you for a tour, princess," I promise, "But I have a few people I want you to meet."

CHAPTER TWENTY-FOUR
arryn

This was a storybook town. That was the only way to describe it, with the bay and the water rolling against the shore, the dramatic cliff edges and sprawling forests. It was lost in time, the buildings having that rustic, old charm to them with boards that hang from the sidings, swinging with a creak as the wind whistles through the town. The roads and sidewalks are uneven, maintained but barely, but it didn't take away from the charm of the place.

We go towards a large house that sits at the edge of the water, the upper floors mostly windows that look out onto the bay. A red truck is parked out front, a stack of logs at the side of the porch and a little dark haired girl is playing out front with a...chicken.

"Is that a chicken?" I whisper hiss at Rett who smirks down at me and gives my hand a squeeze. The warmth of his palm is instantly soothing and for a minute I'm lost to the feel of it. Part of me wants to snatch away from him, but a bigger part is reveling in the stir of emotion that the simple touch provides. I don't pull away and his fingers only firm up, holding me tighter.

"Harper," Rett calls a second later, his face turning soft, his smile brightening. The little girl whips her head up and her eyes go so wide I'm surprised they don't pop out of her head. And then she beams like the first day of summer.

"Uncle Rett!" She squeals, abandoning her chicken and beelining for the man at my side. I tug my hand, ready to give the two of them some space but he doesn't let me go. Instead, he catches the little girl one armed and manages to pull her up, squeezing her in a big hug with her legs kicking and dangling while her arms circle Rett's neck.

"Hey, mini bestie," Rett says to the girl with a full white grin. God he really was devastating. I was stuck on their interaction, how Rett's entire being changed, and all his focus goes to the little girl, except for that one point of contact between us through our linked hands. As if sensing my thoughts, he gives my hand another squeeze as if to remind me he hasn't forgotten I am here. "And how are you?"

"I'm so good!" She says happily. A sudden flurry of movement at my feet has me hopping back, the feathered thing clucking at my toes. "Pickles says hi!" Harper declares.

Rett sets Harper down on her booted feet and the girl

leans down to scoop up the bird, cradling it in her arms, and the chicken literally relaxes as if this was the most normal thing for them.

"You're pretty," Harper gasps, turning her wide eyes on me, "Uncle Rett who's this!?"

"Harper, meet Arryn," Rett says charmingly, "I know she's very pretty, isn't she."

"The prettiest," Harper sways with the chicken, "Is she your girlfriend?"

I can feel my cheeks heating at their attention, my stomach knotting uncomfortably. Everett leans in and whispers something I can't hear, but the little girl giggles with that childlike delight I'm not sure I ever felt as a kid.

She then turns to me with such an innocent open expression my heart stutters in my chest. She didn't look at me like the rest of the world did, didn't see me the way everyone else did, it was innocent and pure and unbiased. I always said I hated kids, didn't like being around them but I'm wondering if that said more about me than it did them. Because they did nothing wrong whereas I have done everything wrong.

Harper is pure where I am marred.

"I want you to meet my momma!" She takes my free hand, "I think you'll really like her."

"You think?" I bend slightly to speak with Harper, smiling at her obvious joy.

The chicken clucks and I back away, a bit of unease blooming towards the bird. But Harper has no problem with it, she pats her head and spins on her heel, skipping toward the house. Our feet crunch across the snow and Rett helps me up the porch steps, so I don't slip on the patches of ice. He doesn't knock, just opens the door, watching as Harper runs on ahead and he guides me through.

The house instantly warms me. It's rustic but modern, with clean accents mixed with more rugged details. It's a home, smelling of coffee and pine, of something feminine and masculine. Toys lay scattered across the floor in the living room, cartoons playing unwatched on the TV above the fireplace while a fire burns steadily beneath it. There were throws on the couches and cushions on the floor, and from the kitchen I could hear the very sweet sound of feminine laughter, mingled with a deep rough chuckle that almost reminds me of Rett.

Letting go of my hand, Rett moves it to my back, almost as if he knows I'll bolt at any minute.

This all seemed very intimate, very close and personal and I wasn't used to that.

We come to a stop in the doorway to a kitchen, something delicious cooking on the stove and I see them.

Two people very obviously in love. She was small, with dark curls and vibrant green eyes, a smile so bright it could rival the sun where he was all dark, dark hair, tanned skin, but his eyes matched Rett's. A dark beard frames his mouth and tattoos cover his skin. He holds the woman close to him, music playing softly as they dance in front of the stove, his large hand framing her waist as he guides her moves, bodies joined at every point they can.

"Momma!" Harper loudly announces her and ultimately our presence, "Look who's here!"

"Rett!?" She gasps but the man she's with just looks pissed. The wedding rings on their fingers show the two of them are married. This had to be Rett's brother.

"Don't stop on our account," Rett drawls, "It's not every day I get to see my older brother doing something other than scowling."

The woman, Maya, I remember Rett calling her from his story, smiles and rolls her eyes, "What are you doing here?"

"Just dropping in to see my favorite person," He ruffles Harper's hair, "Plus I wanted you guys to meet someone."

Rett's brother looks towards us, holding his wife close, protectively, while Harper hovers with the damn chicken in her arms.

"This is Arryn Lauder." Rett gently nudges me, "Arryn this is Torin, my brother, and Maya, his wife, my sister-in-law."

I swallow, "Nice to meet you." I met new people all the time, new faces, names, environments, but I feel out of my element here.

"Blink once for yes, and twice for no," Maya smiles,

"Did Rett kidnap you?"

Her words are in jest, no meaning whatsoever behind them but both brothers go deathly still and so silent, I could hear a pin drop between them.

A few pregnant seconds pass and then Maya gasps, "He *did* kidnap you!?"

"Hey now!" Rett tries but Maya is already moving.

"The fuck, Everett Avery!?"

She clutches my hand protectively, a woman I don't know coming to bat for me.

"I was saving her!" He defends.

"Little doe," Torin steps in, "Just wait a minute,"

"You," She scowls at him, "You knew, and you let him do it!"

"Hey now," He defends but she marches over to him, dragging me along with her, and pokes him in the chest, "Shame on you, Torin Avery."

"Baby, hear him out," Torin says softly, Maya's hand clutching mine.

I didn't know what to say or how to act. I was stumped. My eyes cut to every face in the room, between the innocent eyes of Harper staring on in confusion, to Rett's pleading, Torin's guilt and Maya's fury.

"Are you okay!?" Maya asks me urgently.

"I'm fine," I assure with a swallow.

"What the fuck are you doing?" She growls.

I didn't know what to do here! A woman I didn't know was fully prepared to come to my defense and yet I was finding I didn't want her to. I understood why Rett did what he did, why me, I couldn't fully grasp but I understood.

"It's okay" I find myself saying, "He did it for my own good."

Rett takes a protective step towards me, "It's not that easy."

"You knew," Maya turns her ire to her husband, "You knew about this, and you didn't tell me!"

"There are people after me," I tell Maya, "Everett did what he needed to do to get me out of that situation. He knew I wouldn't come willingly since—" I stop myself from telling them what happened right before my father died. I hadn't forgotten Rett had practically stalked my ass, but they didn't need all the details, "He knew I wouldn't come willingly. I understand now."

"There must have been something else you could have done," She says to Rett, "You kidnapped her."

"Look, let's all calm down for a minute," Torin orders gently.

He looks at his wife like she's his whole world and while Maya was still obviously mad, she softens and accepts his outstretched hand, going to him. Rett slides his arm around my waist. "I'll make coffee," Torin says to us, "Then we can sit down, and you can explain it." He points to Rett.

We agree and while the two of them stay in the kitchen, Rett guides me through to the living room, placing me in front of the fire. "Take off the layers, warm up a little."

I give him a small smile, taking a breath to try ease some of the tension in my muscles.

Alone, I do as Rett suggested and strip off all the outer layers, looking towards the kitchen where Maya and Torin brew coffee. My chest squeezes as I watch them.

I didn't know them but the love between them was so clear and strong it reminded me of the conversation I had with Rett about love stories.

I said the kind of love in romance didn't exist and he'd said it did because he's seen it.

And now, I have seen it too.

CHAPTER TWENTY-FIVE
arryn

The fire blazes in the hearth, warming the room while Torin and Maya sit facing Rett who explains the situation to Maya. I feel her eyes on me, sympathy radiating off her even though she remains silent while the story is told.

Harper is playing with the chicken beyond the windows, the small child bundled up in layers, a hat, almost too big for her head keeps falling over her forehead and every now and then she lifts her gloved hand to push it back up, leaving it askew.

But she was smiling, laughing, her cheeks rosy from the cold, her bright eyes beaming. She was happy.

When I thought of small towns, I thought dreary, boring, a place to come to when you're ready to die. But this place was nothing like that. It was quiet, sure, there were very few people around, but it was *alive*.

And I was starting to realize that a place doesn't need to be packed or teeming with people, it doesn't need big shopping malls or busy highways for it to be a place worth living. This town, these people, this was a home.

Rett startles me when he places his hand on my shoulder, drawing me from my fixation on the window.

"I'm very sorry for your loss," Maya says gently, her eyes soft.

She is truly beautiful, with dark hair and green eyes. A scar slices through her brow and I remember Rett telling me small bits about her and Harper's past, and I know her story is just as tragic as mine.

"Thank you." I swallow, "This is just what I have now."

"Your sister," Torin joins in, "She'll take on the hotel now?"

I nod, "Unless I go back."

"Which you can't do because of the hit. The moment you step foot on the mainland is the moment you sign your death certificate." Torin says.

The words weren't intended to be harsh, but I flinch anyway. "Yes."

"The Ware's, they ordered the hit?" Maya frowns.

"I would assume so, yes. Arryn is the only witness to her father's murder."

"So why don't you fake it?"

My spine stiffens, "What?"

"Fake your death," Maya continues, "Rett takes on the contract, you stage your death, and he sends the images to them. They think you're dead, they take down the mark."

"She'll never be able to go back," Torin says to his wife gently, his hand moving towards her stomach but then he stops himself and drops his hand, rolling his shoulders as if he was about to do something he wasn't supposed to.

Rett didn't appear to notice the sudden shift, but I did.

"Not necessarily," Maya subtly slides her fingers over Torin's hand, "If the Ware's think she is dead, and no longer a problem, they'll come out of hiding. At the moment, they're protecting themselves but when the threat of exposure is gone, there'll be no more reason to hide."

"I'm not following," I say, keeping my focus on the couple ahead of me. Torin and Rett are very similar, but where Torin was rugged, Rett was clean, but they shared the same eye color and hair color. Torin is slightly taller but size wise, they were both broad and fit. Torin's tattoos covered his arms, dark swirls of ink etched expertly into his skin, and I had to wonder if Rett went to the same artist because the ones hidden beneath his clothes looked just as intricately done.

"Well, if they think you're dead," Rett is awfully quiet at my side, he's tense, muscles stiff and I flick my eyes to see a muscle ticking in his jaw. He didn't like talking about me dead, no matter how fake it was but Maya continues anyway, "Rett will be able to take them out when they show themselves again. And then there's no more threat against you."

"That seems too easy," I breathe, "What happens when the world also believes I'm dead?"

"They won't know." Rett speaks quietly.

"The whole world knows I'm missing," I say incredulously, "They'll surely know if I'm dead."

"No," he sighs, "Not if I make your death clean and quiet. The world would never know."

"So, I could go back?"

"Yeah, princess, you could go back if you wanted to. Once it's safe, there would be nothing stopping you from returning to your life if you wanted that."

Hope blooms in my chest at the thought, this sudden overwhelming swell of excitement that I could return to my normal life. I could do my shoots, and run my business. I could have lunch with Suzy and spend my Sundays on the sofa, I could hold my sister's hand and we could say goodbye to my father together. I wouldn't be hiding. I wouldn't be in danger.

I wouldn't be with Rett.

That balloon of hope pops so suddenly, it physically makes me gasp.

I wouldn't be here. On this tiny island, with its snowy peaks and tranquil bay. I wouldn't be in front of a fire. Or drinking coffee while watching the snow.

I would just be Arryn Lauder, heiress and model.

But I'd be with Olivia again, she would no longer be sad and hurt because she thinks something bad has happened to me. The hotel would continue. My father's name would continue and everything he had built would continue.

"I need a minute," I breathe, the list of pros and cons building so long and heavy, I couldn't even figure out what I wanted.

It was stupid for me to let myself believe this is what I wanted. I'd spent barely any time here, had only known Rett a short while, I couldn't lead myself to believe that this was right for me.

My old life was right for me. It had to be since I'd spent the last almost thirty years building it. And if I suddenly change it now, suddenly change everything I thought I wanted, it would have all been for nothing.

It would be a failure.

Rett lets me go but I feel all their eyes on me as I head to the door and let the crisp, winter breeze chase away the sudden heat coursing through me.

I suck in big breaths of the salty air, tune my hearing into the sound of the waves crashing on the shore.

Harper's sweet music like laughter joins with the sound of the ocean and squawking birds, and I just about manage to dodge the chicken as it scurries towards my feet.

"Pickles!" Harper giggles, chasing the bird, "come

here! You have to go back for dinner!"

The bird doesn't listen and continues to run away. But Harper doesn't appear worried, instead she chases it like it's a game they play daily. And never in my life would I have thought a relationship between a girl and chicken could be so damn wholesome, or that chickens apparently made great pets.

I sit on the porch step watching them. Eventually she manages to catch the bird and she cradles it to her chest before she spots me on the porch.

"Hi!" She beams.

"Hello Harper," I smile.

"You look sad, do you need a cuddle?"

My mouth drops open, "Um no, I'm okay."

"Not even from Pickles?"

I cringe at the feathered thing in her arms, "No, really. I'm fine."

She pouts, her brows drawing low over her eyes. She sniffles once before she takes sure steps towards me, determination stamped all over her face. "Here." She doesn't give me a chance to stop her, the bird ends up in my lap and she grabs my wrists, forcing me to hold the bird.

"She likes cuddles," Harper declares fondly, "Just stroke her head."

"I didn't know chickens like to be petted," I say, surprised at the softness of the bird's head under my fingertips.

"Pickles does," Harper sits next to me, "Ruthie said Pickles is like a dog."

"Who's Ruthie?" I question.

"Oh, she lives at the lodge. I love her. She makes the best cookies."

Harper starts talking about everything and nothing, about her school and the town, about the diner that's run by a woman named Imogen and Ruthie's son, Shawn. She throws so much information at me, I find it hard to retain any of it.

"I have to take Pickles to the back now," Harper says.

I pass the chicken over to her, "Thanks."

"Sometimes you just have to talk to someone, so you don't feel sad anymore."

I nod, "You're right."

"Uncle Rett likes to talk too."

CHAPTER TWENTY-SIX
arryn

A headache knocks at my temples, thumping to the beat of my pulse inside my skull. The house is quiet, but I know Torin and Maya are still awake and downstairs in front of the fire. I just needed some painkillers.

Rett sleeps like the dead next to me and I have to lift his arm off my stomach to get out of bed. I creep out of the room and gently pull the door open.

I can hear Torin and Maya's voices, they're whispering so I can't make out what they're saying but I head towards the sound, staying quiet so I don't wake Harper or Rett.

But then I get to the living room, and I pause.

Maya stands in front of the fire, Torin in front of her with his large hand resting across her lower abdomen. She has her hand resting on top of his, her chin angled down with a gentle smile pulling on her mouth.

"Our little bean will be safe," Torin murmurs, "I don't want you to get too involved with what's going on with Everett, little doe."

"We will be fine," she says gently.

"I know you will," he says, "But with everything that happened, I just worry."

"It's not our battle, Torin but I'm not going to leave Rett to handle stuff on his own. He was here when we needed him. He needs us now."

Silence settles between them, but I don't move from my spot. It felt wrong to eavesdrop, but I wanted to see them like this, to see that love burning so brightly between them. It was obvious Maya was pregnant, early on likely and the way Torin cares for her makes my heart feel a little funny.

"I like Arryn," Maya tells him, "I think she'll be good for him."

"Rett falls headfirst into things," Torin sighs, "I don't want to get my hopes up that this won't be one of his fixations that he'll grow bored of."

"Give him his due, Torin," Maya lightly scolds, "He cares for her."

I close my eyes, feeling the sting of tears behind my lids.

"You're right. He does," Torin agrees. "I hope she feels the same."

Not wanting to hear anymore, I purposely clear my throat and walk into the room, making enough noise to notify them of my presence. They stay close together, but Torin removes his hand from her stomach, instead burying them into the pockets of his jeans.

"Arryn," Maya comes towards me, "You okay?"

"Headache," I scrunch my nose up, "I was hoping you had some painkillers."

"Oh sure," She cocks her head for me to follow her through to the kitchen, "Let me just grab some for you."

I stand awkwardly watching as she pulls a box from the cupboard and retrieves a bottle of pills and hands them over. She grabs a bottle of water from the fridge next.

I accept and quickly take two pills.

"It's a lot, isn't it?" Maya says gently, drawing my attention back to her.

"What is?"

She grins, "The Avery Brothers."

I smile at that, "What makes you say that?"

"They're intense," She widens her eyes dramatically, "I swear those men don't know when to stop being overprotective. Torin won't even let me lift a log."

My eyes drop to her stomach before I can stop them, giving away my knowledge of her news.

She places her hand across her stomach, a softness entering her when she does as if she can already picture holding that small bundle in her arms.

"I'm pregnant, not sick," She laughs, "I can lift a log."

"I think that's the universal mode most husbands go into when their wife is expecting," I say, matter of fact, my tone a little icier than I wanted it to be. I didn't want to admit I was jealous. Jealous of what they had.

She cocks her head, picking up everything I wasn't saying, "It's okay." She tells me.

I shake my head, "I'm not so sure anything is ever going to be okay."

"I thought the same thing, Arryn. Before I came here and met Torin, I didn't know how I was supposed to keep living but he showed me. And then I found my family."

"I'm happy for you," I swallow.

Picking up on my reluctance to continue with this train of conversation she heads out of the room but before she leaves, she pauses, "Give it a chance, Arryn. Theres a lot to gain when you let some of those walls down."

"Goodnight," I say to her back, standing alone in the kitchen.

The jealousy left a bad taste in my mouth. I'd never wanted something like this until now.

The door clicks closed behind me, and I suck in a breath before I turn to face the bed. I expect Rett to still be asleep, but instead I find him propped up on the pillows, the sheets pooled around his hips and he's looking at me.

"You okay?" He asks.

"I didn't mean to wake you," I answer.

"You didn't," He smiles gently, pulling back the sheets. I go, climbing into the empty space beside him, "I woke when you got up, but I figured you didn't want to be followed everywhere you go."

"I'm surprised you didn't," I smile into his chest, inhaling that scent that is inherently Rett, like leather and rain, surprisingly comforting, "not worried I'll run away?"

He chuckles and reaches for me, hauling me until I'm straddled over his hips.

It would be so easy to love Everett Avery.

"I don't mind a good chase, little storm, the reward is always so much better when I've had to work for it."

His words rush heat through me. I'm picturing that first day I woke up here, remembering how it felt to be chased and caught by him. Fucking terrifying but exhilarating all the same. And then he'd caught me and pinned me in the snow...

"You want to play that game, princess?" He sits up, pressing our chests together as his hand wraps into my hair. He tugs to expose my throat and then his tongue is sliding up my neck. I shiver at the feel of him, my thighs aching.

When I don't answer him, he gently lifts my hips and slides his fingers under the hem of my new sleep shorts.

"Oh, I think you do," He grins triumphantly when he finds me wet at the mere thought of being chased by him.

What will he do when he catches me? Fuck me right there and then? Up against a tree? On the snowy ground?

It was unlike anything I would ever do before but now, here, I wanted nothing more.

"It makes you wet thinking about it," He continues, working his fingers through my center, spreading the wetness over me. "You like not being in control. You like it when I take you without mercy."

"Yes," I admit, riding his hand.

"Good," He says, "Because I fucking love it when you submit to me, baby. I love being in control of your body."

"Fuck, Rett." I moan, gasping when he circles my clit with his fingers.

"I plan to," He chuckles, "Take off your shorts."

I comply without argument, stripping out of my shorts.

"Now your shirt."

I slide it over my head, leaving myself bare for him.

"Such a good girl." He pinches a hardened nipple between his fingers, "Now take off my boxers and suck my cock."

Jesus Christ.

He lifts his hips so I can slide the white boxers over his muscular thighs, his hard cock jutting up, looking so damn mouthwatering I wanted nothing more than to have it in my mouth. I get between his legs and lean down, fully ready to take him to the back of my throat but he stops me before I can.

"Not like that baby," He pulls me to him, "Turn around and sit your sweet cunt on my face,"

"What!?"

"You heard me," He coaxes me to turn, "There's no way I'm letting a taste go to waste."

"Rett," I say uncertainly.

"Trust me, baby. Do as I ask. You like it when I control this, then give me the control."

Swallowing, I position myself and he immediately swipes his tongue through me. I almost fall from the sensation of it, barely keeping myself upright and moan. Holy shit that feels good.

His hands spread me apart and he doesn't waste a second eating me like a damn man starved. The position meant I was able to lean down and suck the tip of his cock into my mouth, his salty precum hitting my tastebuds.

His moan vibrates against my pussy which in turn makes me pause to revel in the feel of it. Wrapping my hand around the base of him, I take him again into my mouth, swirling my tongue around the underside of his cock which makes his shaft jerk in my hand.

Fingers bite into my flesh as he tries to control himself and focus on the pleasure he's giving me, but I liked doing this. I liked having this tiny ounce of control to make him feel as good as he made me.

"Shit," He groans, coming away from my center to curse, his hips jerking as I slide him to the back of my throat and bob, sucking him until his muscles tense and his fingers bruise.

"Shit, Arryn," He rasps, "Fuck I'm going to come."

I work harder, squeezing my fist around his shaft before I run my hand down and cup his balls.

"Princess," He begs and I grin, sucking him all the way back, his cock jerking in my mouth and then he comes and his climax hits the back of my throat. I continue, swallowing him down as his hips thrust into my mouth, and then let him go with a wet pop of my lips.

I shift slightly and look over my shoulder. His mouth

is glistening with me, and his eyes turn feral when he catches mine.

I open my mouth to speak but before I can, I'm on my back, my legs are over his shoulders and his fingers are buried so far into me I can do nothing but cry out. His tongue works over my clit, his shoulders forcing my legs to remain up.

He fucks me with his fingers and sucks my clit into his mouth until I'm a writhing mess beneath him, fingers clawing at his hair to keep him exactly where he is.

He suddenly curls his fingers, brushing on that sweet, sensitive spot inside and I detonate. I have to grit my teeth to stop from being so loud, the orgasm rattling through me.

There's no reprieve when the orgasm subsides.

Rett crawls up my body, latches his mouth to mine, the taste of me on his tongue as he slides his cock into me on one deep, quick thrust.

CHAPTER TWENTY-SEVEN

everett

I watch Arryn from the bed as she slips into her new clothes. Her hair is tied up in a towel, body fresh from the shower. She's so damn beautiful it hurts.

"What?" She blushes, buttoning the jeans and picking up her sweater, the blue material dangling from her dainty fingers.

"Come here," I order her gently. Laying the sweater down, she sways her hips as she walks towards me, throwing her legs over my hips to straddle me. "I just showered."

"And you smell fucking delicious," I bury my face between the valley of her breasts, covered in a delicate black lace that I try not to remember that my brother picked out.

"You can't seriously want more," she laughs, the

sound of it so carefree it lightens something in my own chest. We'd only stopped an hour ago, I needed to shower but she had to be fucking mad to think I couldn't and wouldn't go again and again with her.

"With you I always want more," I admit, kissing the mound of her breast and then the other, before I kiss my way up her throat and to her jaw. "Are you sore?"

She nods, curling her hand around my neck.

"Good," I grin against her, "Can't have you forgetting about me."

"I'm not sure that would be possible," she breathes.

I kiss her quickly, holding her to me as if to breathe her soul into my body and then let her go. "I need to go to the cabin and get my equipment."

"Okay, do you want me to come?"

"No princess, why don't you spend some time with Maya? She can show you around town if you like."

"Yeah," she smiles, "I'd like that I think."

"You think?" I cock a brow.

"No, I would like that, Rett. I've never been to a place like this before."

I nod, "It's home."

Once I'm ready, I head down to find them all in the kitchen. Harper is telling Arryn about something that happened last week while Maya and Torin listen in. My brother hands me a coffee and knocks my shoulder.

"Maya, would you show Arryn around?" I ask.

"Of course!" Maya agrees quickly, "I have some errands to run first though!"

"That's okay," Arryn says, "It'll be nice to just get out."

Guilt gnaws at my stomach, but it will all be fine soon. It will all be over.

I was trying not to think what that meant for the two of us. I wasn't sure I could simply let her go, not now that the obsession was buried so deep there was no cure for it. I'd wanted her so badly, did morally questionable things to know her, and protect her, that letting her go seemed like an impossibility.

No, not seemed. *Is* an impossibility.

I will follow that woman to the end of the earth and beyond, if I have to.

Arryn leaves with Maya and Harper twenty minutes later and I grab my boots, ready to hike up to the cabin.

"I'll come with you," Torin offers, grabbing his own footwear before we set off.

For the first thirty minutes it's silent between us until the trees swallow us, and the wind picks up in strength, the icy bitterness of it biting at my face.

"Maya's pregnant," Torin tells me.

My feet stop on the craggy incline, and I stare at his back. "Well shit," I grin, "Congratulations, brother."

"I'm fucking terrified," He admits, not stopping at all so I have to pick up speed to catch up.

"Of what?" I ask.

"Keeping them safe."

"This isn't like before, Tor," I say to him, referring to the tragedy that ended with the death of his first wife and infant son.

"No, it isn't," he agrees.

"I won't bring back the trouble here," I assure him, "It's not going to end that way."

He looks over his shoulder to me, "You really care for her."

"Is that such a surprise?"

His mouth cocks up into a smirk, "Yeah, Rett it is. A few months ago, you were trying to rope me in on a job and now it's your life mission to take care of that woman."

"Things change," I grunt, going ahead of him.

"Women do that," He says to my back, "You think you're fine the way you are and then bam, they throw you off course."

"Maya is good for you."

"And it seems Arryn is for you, too."

"If she'll have me." I say, "I'm not so sure our ending will be the same as yours."

Torin doesn't speak again.

I was happy for my brother, he deserved this. Deserved a life with the woman he loved, deserved to be a father to both Harper and this new baby. A few months ago, I would have said it was a shit way to live when we've grown up the way we have, but I know now I was wrong.

I wanted what he had.

"You heard from Kolt?" I ask when we get close to the cabin.

"No. You?"

"Nope." I answer. Our adopted brother had always been elusive, but this was the longest it had been without checking in. It was making me worry something bad had happened. We would know, one way or the other, but it still didn't sit right.

At the cabin I grab what I need and stuff it into my pack. Arryn hadn't agreed to fake her own death yet, but I wanted to be prepared anyway. It was a good idea, and if I could lure the Ware's out of hiding, I could eliminate the threat all together.

I would speak with Arryn when we return, figure out her thoughts on it. I'd need to be quick to get the job when it comes back up so another doesn't get a hold of it and force us to wait longer to get this done.

The sooner I can remove the threat against Arryn, the easier it will be to breathe.

The trek back down the cliff is quiet, the sound of the wind whistling through the pines and the crashing waves the only noise to accompany our journey back to town. The girls still aren't home when we get back to the house, so I set my equipment up in Torin's office, and go looking for them with my brother.

CHAPTER TWENTY-EIGHT
arryn

We walk slowly through the town, both silent as we snack on the fresh pastries we picked up from the bakery. Everyone who sees us greets Maya and gives me a kind smile too, a warm but quiet greeting.

We dropped Harper off a few hours ago at the tiny little school and Maya had given me a tour, from the cemetery all the way back to the docks. Finishing off the pastries, Maya guides me towards the beautiful white building set back and bordered by a sprawling forest of pines. We follow a quaint cobble path, the sound of chickens travelling from the back of the building.

"This is where Harper found Pickles," Maya explains with a humored smile, "It was strange at first."

"I can imagine," I laugh, "I'm not sure what I would have done if my child brought home a chicken as a pet."

She nods her agreement, "Still, I would have given her anything then to make her smile. If that means my daughter keeps a chicken, then a chicken it is."

The door opens ahead of us and an older woman steps onto the wrap around porch. Kindness oozes from every inch of the woman, dark eyes, hair and skin, she smiles brightly at Maya, wiping her hands on a dish towel.

"My sweet," she wraps Maya into a tight hug like it had been weeks since they last saw each other, but I doubted it had been that long. There was a fondness in the way the woman looks at Maya, motherly almost, so I had a feeling her greetings were always that warm.

"Hi Ruthie," Maya squeezes the woman's hand before she turns to me, "This is Arryn, Everett's…" she trails off and cocks a brow, a knowing smile pulling on her mouth.

"Friend," I insert, swallowing it down. We were much more than friends – lovers? Friends who fuck? In a relationship? I had no fucking idea.

"Oh, good lord," Ruthie blows out a breath, "Good luck to you, sweetness, he's certainly something."

I laugh in shock, "He sure is."

"Come in," She ushers us through, "I swear another snowstorm is about to come in."

I step through the door to instant warmth and comfort, there's the smell of fresh bread wafting through, mixed with coffee and logs burning. It was a lodge of some sort, cozy and quaint and incredibly quiet.

"We get busier in the spring and summer," Ruthie explains, "It's not always this dull."

"I think it's lovely," I say honestly. Paintings hang on the walls, an array of different scenes that all resemble the small little town, from the bay to the buildings that haven't stepped out of time.

Ruthie pats my hand, "Sit down, the two of you, I'll fetch coffee."

"She never stops," Maya rolls her eyes, "I try, but she swats at me like I'm fly if I get in her way."

"She loves you deeply," I observe.

Maya nods, "She does. Harper and Torin too. Even Rett when she can stop complaining about his antics."

"I take it he caused trouble?"

"He has a great skill of winding people up." Maya laughs.

There was not a shred of doubt that that was not true. Playful and charming. My cheeks heat and I look away quickly, picking at the chipped polish on my nails.

Maya doesn't call me on it and I'm grateful for that and when Ruthie returns, another woman is with her.

About Maya's age, with long wavy blonde hair woven with darker honey and caramel-colored strands. And on her hip is a dark-haired boy, no older than two with this mane of dark curls that fall around his round face. He didn't look like the woman holding him in anything but his eyes. Big and round, the color of whiskey and framed by lush dark lashes.

"Vanessa," Maya jumps up and takes the small boy who giggles in delight at her attention.

Vanessa holds her hand to me, and I take it quickly, "Arryn," I introduce myself.

"All the Avery boys are getting themselves together, it seems," She smiles but a sadness enters her eyes that I'm not entirely sure she realizes is there.

Ruthie places the tray with four cups on it on the counter, a fresh pot of coffee steaming in the middle. There's a plate of cookies and a small jug of cream and sugar.

"So how did you meet Rett?" Vanessa asks, giving her finger to the boy for him to wrap his own chubby ones around it.

"He took on a job for my father," Vanessa's eyes widen, and I realize Maya and me aren't the only ones who know exactly what it is the Avery's do. "And it kind of went wrong." I cringe, leaving it at that.

Maya gives me a small sympathetic smile, passing a cookie to the little boy in her arms.

"Is he yours?" I ask Vanessa.

At this she beams, "He is. This is Ethan."

Conversation falls easily and we talk about everything and nothing in between, I tell them about the lingerie I help design and create while Vanessa tells me about college. She was studying to become a doctor but since Ethan was born, she hasn't been able to do much. She was now permanently back on the island after her last trip made her miss home. She told me she wanted this place to be where her son grew up and on her last visit, she had left her son with friends, but it felt wrong to be so far from him. I could only imagine how that must feel, to leave a part of yourself behind. I open my mouth to ask more but the door behind us opens abruptly, banging so hard against the wall it rattles the picture frames.

"It's a door, Everett," Ruthie is already scolding, "Not a barricade, it opens like any other."

"Lovely to see you too, my dear Ruthie."

She rolls her eyes, but a smile pulls on her lips, "Delinquents."

Despite the words, Rett walks over to her and kisses her on the cheek in greeting before he steps towards me, and his hand finds the small of my back. "Did you enjoy the tour?"

"This town is so pretty," I sound almost dreamy when I say it.

His hand goes to my hair, and he strokes it down, fingers scratching at my scalp almost enough to make me purr. I had a newfound love for someone – namely him – playing with my hair.

Torin sticks close to Maya, his hand immediately finding her abdomen.

It felt like family here, a home, even for me, an outsider.

We end up at the diner where I meet even more people, Imogen and Shawn run the single diner in town. We're all squidged into a little booth, the laughter from the table so loud it overpowers the juke box that plays old country in the corner. It was dim but warm and smelled of fried food and beer.

Everything had become a comparison to before, and this was another one. I would never have stepped foot in a place like this back on the mainland, though there were plenty of them and they'd always seemed like so much fun, but it was bad for my image.

But here I wasn't Arryn Lauder, the heiress. I was just Arryn, and I could enjoy a beer and some fried food if I wanted to.

Harper coos at Ethan who throws more food on the floor than he puts in his mouth. Rett sits by my side, his hand on my back but his focus has been elsewhere since we arrived. I follow his eyeline to see him focused on the boy, his brows pulled low in thought, an emotion I can't name twisting his face.

"Are you okay?" I lean in and whisper.

He turns to me quickly, flicking his eyes back to the child one last time, "I'm fine." He says but a week spent in close proximity to him gives me some knowledge to know that he was lying.

Something uneasy twists in my stomach, turning sour incredibly suddenly.

I pick up my beer and down the contents in a few gulps. "Are *you* okay!?" Rett chuckles in disbelief.

"Just fine," I squeak, "Perfectly fine. Can I get another one?" I ask the passing server.

"Sure!" She chirps cheerily.

By the time we've called it a night and are heading back to Torin's house I'm tipsy. Okay I'm drunk. My legs wobble under me but Everett holds me up, laughing when I stumble and slur.

"I've got you princess," he whispers, "I won't let you fall."

I may have spiraled a little with the thoughts, "Is he yours?" I blurt.

"Is who mine, little storm?"

Torin and Maya are further ahead, Harper holding her mother's hand, the picture of a perfect, cute little family.

My brows draw down, "Ethan."

"Vanessa's son!?" He gasps.

"Unless there's another," I hiccup, "Ethan."

He's silent at my side and that does not help one bit. I mean if I really think about it, the boy has his dark hair, it wasn't impossible.

"I mean it's okay," I continue on a slur, "Having a kid."

"Ethan isn't mine, princess."

"Well, how do you know that? I saw you looking."

"For Ethan to be mine," He stops us, pulling me to face him. His face swims in my vision, moving and swirling, making me feel a bit sick. "I would have had to sleep with Vanessa, and I can assure you, I have not been in her bed, nor she in mine."

"Oh."

"Yeah, oh, baby," he affectionately taps my chin with his knuckle.

"But you were looking," I whisper.

"He reminds me of someone is all, Arryn, he isn't mine. I didn't know Vanessa had a child; she's kept it a secret."

"Well now I feel silly."

"Were you jealous, little storm?" I see his three faces smile.

"No," I pout but then my stomach swirls, "Oh god."

Rett is quick to move my hair out of the way as I promptly throw up the beer and food I'd consumed in abundance earlier.

So now instead of just feeling stupid because of my assumption, I now feel like shit too.

CHAPTER TWENTY-NINE
arryn

My head is pounding when I wake the following morning, more sickness swirling in my stomach. Dear god, beer hangovers are worse than wine hangovers.

I have this god-awful taste on my tongue, but I also feel greasy and bloated. Rolling with a groan from the mattress I don't remember falling on, I clamber to the bathroom, dropping to my knees to retch over the toilet bowl. There wasn't anything in my stomach to get up, but it didn't stop my body from trying.

When I'm sure I'm not about to throw up a kidney, I'm finally able to relieve my bladder and groan at the sight of blood.

It really isn't my morning. Hungover, day one of a

period and a headache that made me feel like someone was trying to carve through my skull. I search the bathroom for some sort of pad or tampon I can use, but the drawers are empty and there are no containers on the sides.

"Shit."

"Princess?" I hear Rett call through the closed bathroom door.

"Uh," I stutter, pressing on my temple as if to stop the pounding on my skull. I roll up tissue to pad out my underwear, hoping to save it from a stain, I mean we've all been there, haven't we? And pull them up, opening the door to find Rett with a glass of water and a bottle of pills.

I almost forget about the disaster about to happen in favor of that water but then stop abruptly, "What is it?" Rett immediately asks.

"I started my period."

He softens, "Wait here, princess." He places the items down and leaves the room, only to return a moment later with both a pad and a tampon in hand. I take both, "Thank you." I breathe.

"I'll run to the store to get more, run a bath, and take the pills, I'll be back in ten."

I'm in the tub when Rett returns, placing a fresh

packet of pads on the side, along with a box of tampons, "Sorry, I didn't know which ones you preferred."

"No, this is great, thank you."

He sits on the toilet lid. I'd taken the pills and downed the water like I hadn't had hydration in days, and then desperately tried to keep them down while the tub filled with water. Thankfully I managed it and the headache had passed.

The bubbles I put in the tub pop around my ears and my brow sweats from how hot it is, but it was making me feel better so if I had to stew here for another hour, then I would. Anything to get rid of this hangover and delay any period cramps.

"While I like jealousy on you, princess," Rett leans forward and rests his elbows on his knees, grinning at me playfully, "Next time tell me so I can save you from alcohol poisoning."

I roll my eyes, "I wasn't jealous."

His laugh bounces off the tiles back at me, "If it helps, princess, if I thought you'd slept with a man we were having dinner with, his head would have likely ended up on his plate."

I cast my eyes over to him, and while he still smiles at me, I can see he was deadly serious.

"Yes well, you can't kill all of them, some of them work for the hotel I own."

It was a low blow, but the smile drops from his face

and for a minute I feel better because at least it isn't me he is teasing.

But then it melts away and I huff, "That was a joke, Rett."

He quirks a brow and drops his eyes down to where my body is hidden by the fluffy white bubbles on top of the water, before he gets up and walks towards me. He perches on the edge of the tub.

"I like you a little possessive, princess," He tucks a wet strand of hair behind my ear.

"I'm sorry," I say to him, "I acted…"

"Don't apologize," He says sternly, "You're human."

I lean into his touch, "I like it here."

He smiles and then he washes my hair like the damn unicorn he is.

"We'll do it," I say to Rett at lunchtime. He braided my hair after the bath, and I play with the end of it now.

"Are you sure?" He says.

"Yeah," I agree, "I want to see my sister."

"Okay," he breathes, "I'll claim the job when it comes up again."

I wondered how we would do it. Fake my death. It was hard to think of since it stepped so close to reality. One wrong move for us would land with my death and faking it almost seemed like we were tempting fate.

But this was the quickest way for me to get back to my sister.

Not my life. Not any of it. Just my sister.

I'd watched the news earlier, saw her appeal, I'd lost count of how many she'd made for my safe return. The police had no trace of me, they had no leads on my father's murderers, no leads on anything. My face was plastered across the internet, lists of my 'achievements' like a grocery receipt stamped beneath both old and new model photographs. There was nothing personal noted, except the fact that they liked to point out I was chronically single.

I'd made the mistake of looking at forums and on social media, but I'd seen one scathing post and promptly left that. I didn't need to see that.

But I had seen photos taken unaware of my sister and she looked a mess. Tired and worn down, dark shadows from days of no sleep, her usually tan complexion pale and thin. She looked sick. Exhausted.

Grief was eating her alive.

Right now, she hadn't just lost her father, she had lost me too.

She was the only Lauder standing and it was killing her.

CHAPTER THIRTY
arryn

Arryn is still in the shower when I come up, the sound of the water running spilling in to the room from the slight crack in the door.

Slipping out of my clothes I walk into the steamy room, the scent of honey and lavender saturating the warm air. Her back is to me, long black hair falling down the length of her back, the water running rivers over her curves. I step in behind her, my hands finding her slim waist before they travel up and around to her breasts.

"Rett," She breathes, leaning back against me. I kiss her neck, the hot water soaking me as I line my body up with hers. I should be alarmed at how easy it is for her to unravel me.

"We can't," She mumbles, stifling a moan when I

pinch her nipples between my fingers.

"Why not?"

"I'm bleeding," She curls her fingers around my wrists, stopping me from moving them.

"I'd be in the wrong line of work if I was afraid of a little blood, princess," I keep toying with her sensitive breasts, watching as goose bumps chase over her skin, despite the heat from the shower. "We're in the shower, it'll wash away."

Her fingers grow lax, and I pull away from her grip, sliding my hand down the softness of her stomach and to that warm, inviting space between her legs.

I work through her folds, teasing and toying with her until she's a writhing mess in front of me, her ass pushing back onto the hardness of my cock.

"You make me crazy," She moans, her head rolling back to rest on my shoulder.

"The feeling is mutual, little storm," I steal her mouth with mine, forcing my tongue between her lips as I spear two fingers into her.

"Oh god," she cries, "You should stop, Rett, the blood."

I look down to see red streaks snaking down her inner thighs, much lighter in color since it's diluted by the water but it's there.

"I don't care," I assure her.

"I just..." She breathes, "No one has ever."

"Do *you* want me to stop?" I pause my hand; I mean it was entirely possible she was uncomfortable with this, and I didn't want to push boundaries with her.

"Well, no," She tells me with a slight shake in her tone, "it's periods are, you know…"

"Know what?" I laugh, "A completely normal and natural part of a woman's life?"

"You really don't care?" She laughs in disbelief, so I prove it to her. I keep my fingers moving inside of her, pressing my thumb to her clit and circling it slowly.

"Oh," She stutters, throwing out an arm to steady herself as her knees buckle. I chuckle, grinning against her neck as I keep pleasuring her, using my hand to play her body like she was my very own instrument, and I was the only master who knew how it worked.

"Nothing will ever stop me from worshipping you, little storm," I whisper in her ear, my voice a rasp that's almost swallowed by the sound of the water running from the shower.

"Rett, I'm going to come," She moans.

"Good, let me have it," I demand, putting more pressure to her clit and feeling it when she ultimately detonates. Her cry bounces off the tiles, playing like a sweet symphony in my head.

But I wasn't done with her.

I *need* her. Spinning her, I grasp the backs of her thighs and lift, pushing her back against the tiles and thrust, entering her warm, wet body swiftly.

I grunt at the sensation of her body stretching to fit me, as my cock fills her entirely. Her nails claw at my shoulders, biting through my skin to leave it raw and bleeding. But I took the pain and gave it back in pleasure, thrusting into her hard and fast. My fingers sink into the flesh of her thighs as I hold her up the wall, the slickness of the tile aiding her body as it moves with each pump of my hips.

"You feel so fucking good, princess," I groan, looking down between our bodies, watching my cock disappear into her body. "Your cunt was made for me, you know that?"

"Yes," She cries.

"All of you was made for me," I tell her, "Every perfect inch of you."

"Rett," Her nails claw harder.

"Are you going to come for me princess?"

"Please," She begs.

"Hold on to me," I order.

Her arms wind around my neck and her thighs tighten on my waist, allowing me to let go of one thigh to slip a hand between us, putting my attention back to her clit to push her over the ledge once more. She shatters against me, forcing my own climax from me.

I spill into her, filling her with me as she continues to clench and contract around me.

Arryn slumps against my shoulder, breathing hard.

Gently, I unhook her legs and help her to standing, keeping her steady while she gets her bearing.

"There's a mess," She breathes.

I just chuckle and pick up a sponge and some soap. Lathering it up, I begin to swipe it over her skin, careful as I place it between her legs to wash away the blood. And when that's done, I guide her out the shower, wrapping her in a warm towel.

"Go lay down, I'll be there in a moment."

With a dreamy kind of smile on her face, she kisses me and goes into the bedroom, leaving me to wash myself quickly and join her.

She's laying in the bed on her side, her hands cradling under her cheek as she watches me.

"Thank you," She whispers.

"What for?" I cock my head.

"Everything, Everett. For protecting me. For helping me."

I kneel on the bed and lean down, tenderly moving a strand of dark hair from her face. "Always, princess, though I kinda miss you trying to kill me."

She grins, a full smile that shows her pearly white teeth and puts a pretty sparkle in her stormy eyes.

When I lay down beside her, she curls into my chest, her hand settling over my heart.

"What happens when this is all over?" She whispers.

The light I'd left on gives the room a cozy kind of glow. The snow has stayed away, and it's started to melt, though I doubt it will stay away for long.

"What do you want to happen?" I ask.

I hold my breath waiting for her answer, praying it would match mine. There was no way I could leave her.

"I'm so confused," She admits. "And I feel guilty."

"What about?"

"I want to stay," she whispers as if saying it out loud would be too much, too real.

"Here?"

Arryn nods, and her throat bobs against me as she swallows. "But staying means abandoning everything from before. The hotel, my sister…"

"But what about you?" I ask.

She shrugs, "I don't know."

"I'm not going anywhere," I tell her, "Whatever choice you make, I'll follow you."

"There's those stalking tendencies," she teases but it falls flat.

"I mean it, princess. I will follow you to the end of the earth and beyond if you so asked me to."

CHAPTER THIRTY-ONE
arryn

Three days had passed since we came down from the cabin in the woods. It hadn't taken long to fall into a rhythm with these people and it was so easy too. Maya and I walked in the morning while we took Harper to school, and then we stopped at Ruthie's for coffee and Vanessa joined us.

I barely know Vanessa, and yet I felt a kind of friendship with her blooming that hadn't occurred for me before. Suzy was different, I loved her like a sister, but that friendship started because I paid her, this one, it was starting from me simply being well... *me*.

I hold little Ethan in my arms, he's only just turned two and the cutest little bundle I've ever met. He's currently pulling on a strand of my hair with one hand, one of Ruthie's oat cookies in the other, crumbs stuck to his chin and cheeks.

Vanessa hadn't mentioned anything about Ethan's father, and I hadn't asked since it was none of my business, but I had a feeling it was a sore subject for her anyway.

She was visibly wary of both Torin and Rett, and I couldn't help but notice that she had a habit of shielding Ethan from them both, not well but she tried.

It pulled on my curiosity, but I wouldn't pry for information she wasn't willing to give.

She was a kind woman, smart, beautiful with so much love for her family and this island. She gave up her studies to take care of her son, which I respected but it also made my heart twinge with sadness. If the father was in the picture perhaps, she would have that time for her education, have that time to follow her dreams.

But that's the sad thing about single mothers, it is often their dreams that are sacrificed. It doesn't make the love for their children any less, doesn't make *them* any less but it happens, and people overlook that sacrifice.

I stare down at Ethan's happy little face, gaze into those young, innocent eyes and wonder what kind of mother I would be. I'd never thought about having children, I didn't have time but now, could I do it? Could I have a little boy of my own? Would he have dark curls and icy eyes like Rett? Or would it be a daughter?

"I know that look," Maya slides up next to me, offering her finger to Ethan which he accepts in favor of my hair.

"Sorry?" I ask.

"The way you're looking at him," Maya says, cooing at the boy, "You want children."

I smile, "Maybe one day."

"You and Rett would make such cute babies," She whispers as if in conspiracy, "But don't tell him I said that."

"Rett and I, I'm not sure we're built to last like you and Torin are." I admit.

"I've seen the way he looks at you, Arryn," she scoffs, "That man looks at you like you hung the moon and stars. Hell, he looks at you like you built the whole damn universe. He's halfway in love with you, if he's not there already."

"We barely know each other."

"There are no rules when it comes to love Arryn, I learned that."

"How did you and Torin meet?"

"I was running," she accepts Ethan into her arms when he gives her grabby hands and bounces him on her hip, "My ex was abusive, always had been but it got so bad, and he almost killed me. I ran and tried to steal a ride on Torin's boat back to the island."

"I'm so sorry," I mumble, horrified at her words. How could anyone want to hurt Maya? She was so sweet, so good, it was pure evil.

"Torin and I didn't really get along when I came here. I guess stowing away on his boat didn't help much but after some time we just…clicked and everything happened. And now, I couldn't imagine being without him. He's my sun and moon. It didn't come without challenges," she tells me, cradling the back of Ethan's head as he settles in ready to take a nap, "just like I'm sure you and Rett will face them. But sometimes, when things are just meant to be, it'll work out."

"You're very optimistic," I smile at her, sighing.

"Life's a little sad without those silver linings."

I nod and say no more, staring down at the coffee in my mug.

"Let me give you some advice," Maya touches my shoulder gently, "Open your mind to a life beyond what you've been taught and what you know. When you do, you'll realize there is so much more waiting for you."

I watch Maya wander off to Vanessa, a sleeping Ethan in her arms and I take a seat on one of the plush couches in front of a large fireplace, the flames crackling and hissing up the chimney. There was a light and quick snowfall this morning, but it hadn't lasted long, though the clouds were rolling and tumbling, the threat of more to come soon.

"Need some alone time?" Ruthie has a voice anyone could recognize, kind and warm, instantly soothing. She sits by me on the couch with a groan, rolling her eyes when I cast my eyes to her in concern, "Don't look at me like that, miss Arryn, I'm old but I'm not *that* old. The cold messes with my joints."

"And yet you live on an island that's always cold."

"Not always," she knocks my knees, "Spring and summer are wonderful, warm. The island comes alive with the sun."

"This really is a little story book town, isn't it." It made me feel like a little girl reading a fairy tale, getting lost in those pages where dragons soared through the skies and battles were won and lost, princesses falling in love with the heroes. I missed my books, my stories. They were a comfort, but I had to admit this little island gave me the same feeling as if I was reading it from the pages of my favorite books.

"It is," Ruthie agrees, "This has been my home for many good years. I've seen it house heartbreak, tragedy, love, it tells stories and holds many secrets in the old walls. But why are you here, Arryn? What will this little town do for you?"

I roll my lips, "I wish I knew the answer." I tell her. She sits with me for a moment, the silence settling between us comfortable as the fire continues to blaze ahead of us. Eventually though, she has to go back to work, so I get up and head back to Rett. There are so many unanswered questions rolling around inside my head, and I know Rett can answer them if I only had the courage to ask.

The cold salty air bites at my face, the wind rolling off the sea to tangle up my hair as I walk the short way to Torin's house. A sense of calm moves through me with the sound of the waves and the birds, there's no loud horns or shouting, no flashing cameras or enraged customers to deal with. Just the sea, the sky, and the forest.

I was living each day with anxiety weighing down my shoulders but here, I didn't feel an ounce of that as I walked, my feet crunching over frozen grass towards Rett who helps chop wood with Torin outside the waterside house.

Despite the chill, both were just in t-shirts, muscles flexing and rolling with each swing of the axe. Sweat soaks Rett's chest and rolls down his temples but there is a deep frown marring his face, an anger twisting his mouth and when he slams that axe down on the wood, it's with purpose and rage.

Something has pissed him off and that poor piece of wood stood no chance against it.

His eyes are instantly on me when my foot snaps a twig.

The lines of anger smooth, his whole body softening towards me.

"Hi," I smile.

He takes three strides towards me, one more to secure our bodies together with a strong arm around my waist and then his lips are on mine in a possessive, all-consuming kiss. He melts me, my body relaxing into his, the taste of salt hitting my tongue as he deepens the kiss.

His fist curls into my hair, pinning me to him.

I manage to break the kiss, breaths heavy and puffing out of us in white clouds that form in front of my mouth. "What's wrong?"

"Your hit was released today," He kisses the corner of my mouth, sadness drooping his shoulders, "I claimed it."

"It's okay," I stroke the back of his head.

"No, princess, it's not!" He snaps, stepping back from me. "It's not fucking okay!"

"Everett," I step towards him.

"I fucking hate this!" he growls loud enough to draw Torin's attention. "I hate that my name is currently headlining your death warrant. I fucking hate that I have to be the one to do it, despite how fake it is. I hate that I'm going to pose you as dead, cover you in blood and force you to lay there like you're not breathing. It plays on my mind because there's this damn line that makes this fiction a reality. If something goes wrong, I lose you. And I cannot lose you little storm."

"Rett," I close the gap between us before he can step away from me and let his thoughts and fears consume him. My hands cup his face, eyes meeting his, there is so much strength in him, so much loyalty but woven into those threads is fear. Fear for me. "You're not going to lose me. You're not."

"Arryn," His forehead presses onto mine, his breath whooshing from his lungs as if in defeat, "Princess."

"This is just the start, Rett," I tell him, "This is just

the start to making it go back to normal. To making it go away. We can't live in the woods for the rest of our lives. That is no life. We would be looking over our shoulders forever, running when our secret slips. We can't have a future if we're trapped in the past."

"You want a future?"

"With you? Yes. But not like this."

"Not like this," he repeats, "I will protect you, Arryn, you have my word."

"I know, Rett." I kiss him, "I know."

CHAPTER THIRTY-TWO

arryn

Everett was tortured.

It didn't matter what I said, how much I told him it was okay, that it wasn't real, it ate at him. He'd barely spoken a word since I returned earlier, not to me, to Torin or Maya. Even little Harper couldn't get him out of his head.

This is hurting him.

Before, I knew Everett cared for me, liked me even, but now I'm wondering how deep his feelings for me go.

It didn't matter how fictional my death was going to be, even just implying it, was enough to send him over the edge.

And I got it, I did, but this was the means to an end.

This was the right thing for us to do.

I take the mug of coffee over to where Rett sits in front of the fire, the day now turned to night, a clear moonless sky which allows all the brilliant twinkling stars to shine against the velvety black night. The ocean is calm, gently lapping at the shore and though it is cold, there are no storms or snow.

I didn't much believe in omens but the fact that we had a calm night ahead of us seemed like a good thing.

His eyes bounce to me before I've approached and he runs them down my body, not in desire or even lust but in protectiveness. As if something terrible could have happened to me in the last ten minutes.

His hand curls around the back of my jean clad thighs as I place the coffee down on the table and then he pulls me into his lap, wraps his arms tightly around my waist and buries his face into my hair. He inhales deeply, his muscles seeming to loosen now that I was in his arms.

I thread my fingers into the thick hair at the back of his head.

"Can we go back to the cabin?" I ask quietly, my voice almost lost to the crackle and pop of the flames in front of us. "I think I want to do this with only us."

He nods slowly, "Yeah, princess we can."

"It's not real," I whisper, "We're okay."

He just tightens his arms more and doesn't say a word

and when we go to bed that night, he holds me the entire time. There isn't a second where some part of him isn't touching some part of me and even in sleep, his worries still claim him. The deep set of his frown, the downturn of his lips which almost made him look like he was in pain, told me his dreams were not being kind.

When we wake the following morning neither of us look well rested.

His hand smooths down the back of my black hair and he kisses my forehead before he finishes packing a bag for us to take to the cabin.

We would only be there for a few days since more snow was forecasted. He said it would be safer for us to stay in town where we can still access all the necessities we will need.

I also think he likes giving me the company of his brother and Maya. And I appreciated that. I'd been so lonely without realizing it, and the last few days spent with his family and friends has given me something I didn't know I needed.

I hug Maya before we set off and Harper surprises me when she rushes over to wrap her little arms around my middle, her rosy cheek pressing into my stomach.

"How long!?" She asks.

"How long for what, sweetheart?"

"How long will you be gone?" She looks up at me with her big, innocent eyes.

"Only a couple days," I assure her, "Don't worry, your uncle Rett will be back in no time."

"Rett always comes back," She dismisses, "But I was scared you wouldn't."

My heart does a weird little gallop in my chest. "I'm coming back," I promise, "Thank you for being my friend, Harper."

Rett gives Harper a kiss on the head before we both leave, and though this was what I wanted, this was the right thing, every step I take away from the town, I can't help but feel like I was leaving a part of me behind. The trees swallow us, the wind chills us but it wasn't just externally I felt cold, it was like my blood was cold too.

I can't shake the feeling, can't even place what it is that I am feeling but it remains, like heavy metal in the pit of my stomach.

Rett helps me up the cliffside, aiding me over large, slippery rocks that jut out of the earth and over downed trees. I don't remember it being this dangerous on the way down, but we manage it, my lungs burning from the exertion of the climb. While most of the snow had melted over the last few days, some remained in the darkest parts of the forest, where the sun can't touch it.

After a couple hours of hiking, I glimpse the tiny little cabin buried in the woods. My breath whooshes from me and a smile touches my lips.

"Never thought I'd come to love this place," I laugh, squeezing Rett's hand.

"It has a certain appeal," He quirks a brow at me playfully, "I like it more now that you're in it."

"That's just because you can fuck me against every surface," I tease, lightening the somber mood that saturates us, "No one around to catch us after all."

Some light has reentered Everett during the hike up, his shoulders don't appear as tense. I doubt he's happy accepting the path we have chosen, but it doesn't seem to be weighing on him as much now that it was just us here.

"Every surface," he steps closer, "In front of every window, on the porch, against a tree…" his finger curls beneath my chin, "And it doesn't matter how loud you scream, the only ones to witness my destruction of you are the trees and the sky, and I think they like your pretty screams."

An ache blooms in the pit of my stomach as his words travel their way through me. Heat burns in his gaze and his mouth notches up at the side in a knowing smirk, eyes dipping down to where I press my denim clad thighs together, his words painting a vivid picture.

"You know how I love when you submit to me, princess, how needy your perfect little cunt is. I like destroying you for any other man. You are mine."

"Yours," I agree.

"Then run, little storm," he whispers it so quietly I almost miss it, but then his words register.

"What?"

"I'm going to earn what's mine today," he wraps a strand of my dark hair around his finger and tugs, "don't think I don't remember how you told me you liked it when I chased you. You've been such a good girl giving yourself to me like you have, you simply proved you've been mine all along but today, right now, little storm, I am going to earn you."

He drops the bag and kicks it beneath a tree and out of view. I doubted anyone would be up here, but he was taking precautions.

The cabin was right there but he didn't want to move from this spot and the little bubble he's just put us in.

"And when I catch you," he purrs, leaning in to brush his lips across mine, sending an explosion of butterflies to take flight in my stomach, "I'm going to claim you. Fuck you raw until you can't even stand." His hand cups me, the heel of his palm pressing against the most sensitive part of me. "*When* I catch you, there will be no doubt about who you belong to. Mine to fuck, please, dominate and worship. So run, little storm, time is ticking."

Holy shit. This was happening.

"How can you be so sure you'll catch me," I breathe, taking a few paces back, my eyes remaining on his face which was set in primal dedication to this little game we are playing.

"I'm one of the best trackers to exist, I've been trained to find pretty things like you. This is no different, my beautiful little storm. I'll count to thirty and then I'm coming for you."

I'm running before the first number has left his lips.

"One, two, three…"

Adrenaline courses through my body, both fear and arousal fraying my nerves and setting me on fire. I use trees and branches to propel myself forward, burying myself further into the woods. The light of day dims when the canopy above me becomes thicker, the smell of damp earth and sea salt becoming so pungent here I almost choke on it.

"Ten, eleven, twelve…" His voice carries through the trees, rough with desire.

Still, I run, my voice trapped in my throat. I couldn't tell you if I wanted to laugh or scream.

"Eighteen, nineteen, twenty…"

His voice disappears the further I get until I can no longer hear him. He must have gotten to thirty now, but I'm breathing so loud, my feet even louder, that I couldn't hear anything other than myself. He could be behind me; he could be close.

And though I wanted him to catch me, I also wanted to make him work. To earn it, like he so graciously said.

The blooming heat in my core isn't helping my grace, I'm clumsy and inelegant as I clamber over rocks and branches, making sure to pay attention to the ground so I don't accidently impale myself on any of the sharp, merciless rocks that jut out from the ground.

"I can hear you, little storm," His voice is both near

and far, an echo through the trees that keeps coming. "It's like you want this to be over already. Are you that desperate, princess?"

I couldn't tell where he was and I swing my head around, trying to catch a glimpse of him but all I see are trees and shadows.

A little nervous laugh bubbles out of me and I jump over another rock, grabbing hold of a tree to stop my forward motion and swing behind it, pressing my back against the rough bark as my chest heaves with my breaths.

His chuckle sounds. He was close, so fucking close.

I could end this now. Reveal myself to him but I think he expects that from me.

And I didn't mind proving Everett Avery wrong.

I knew he would catch me but that didn't mean I had to make it easy.

I belonged to him but the end of this was his reward and rewards only come to those who work for it.

CHAPTER THIRTY-THREE

everett

My breathing comes out in easy, calm breaths, my steps sure and careful. Not a branch snaps or a rock moves as I stalk through the trees.

I hear the wind, the sea, the birds high up in the branches but more importantly, I hear her, can visibly see the path she has taken.

There are snapped branches, tracks where her boots have left prints in the wet earth. She moves noisily away from me, her adrenaline giving her speed but not grace.

I grin, "I can hear you, little storm," I say it loud enough that it travels through the trees, "It's like you want this to be over already. Are you that desperate princess?"

More snapping of branches and then a sweet little

laugh that's so quiet I almost miss it.

And then silence.

Clever girl.

Chuckling, I keep moving silently through the woods. We haven't ventured too far into the woods, but it was denser here, the light dimmer since the sun couldn't penetrate the canopy above.

I listen carefully, waiting for another snap from a branch, the crunch of rocks moving while my eyes watch every shadow for movement.

I was already fucking hard, desperate for my little storm. My fingers ached to be holding her, to be buried in her hair, my lips on her skin.

Sudden movement to the left has me swinging that way, ducking low to remain unseen but I have my eyes on her now. She moves quickly through the trees, softer and quieter than she was before, her nimble body working beautifully, and I lose sight of her as she dips into the shadows.

"I can almost taste how fucking perfect you are," I call out, "I bet your greedy little pussy is begging to be filled. Are you wet, princess?"

She stumbles, the sound of scraping shoes and air rushing out of her lungs hits my ears. For a second, I worry she's fallen and hurt herself, but she doesn't cry out nor does she stop moving. It was only a matter of time before I catch her.

"I can't wait to feel you dripping all over my cock," I

keep talking, teasing her with my words, "so wet as I slide into you so deep, you'll feel me there for a week."

She was up ahead, to the right and hidden behind a tree. So still and silent I'm sure she believes I'm never going to find her.

Dropping back, I step further into the density of the forest, using the shadows to my advantage as I stalk up to her, quiet and deadly. I see her right ahead of me, looking in the other direction.

She moves slowly to peer around the tree and that's when I strike.

I lunge for her, gripping her by the back of the neck to spin her and press her chest against the tree.

She screams as I pin her there, grinding my cock into the curve of her ass.

"You've been teasing me with these tight as fuck jeans," I rasp in her ear, reveling in her little whimper as I grind against her again, letting her feel how fucking hard I am for her right now. "Running through the woods like you actually want to escape me, but we both know you don't."

"Everett," she moans, fingers curling into the tree as if she is trying to claw the bark right off.

"Are you wet, princess?" I growl, inhaling the scent of her hair, "Do you ache?"

"Yes," she pushes back against me, "Don't make me wait."

"Needy little thing," I praise, "I want to fill you up. Lose myself to you. Have I earned you now, baby?"

"I'm yours," she looks over her shoulder, lids hooded over her pretty eyes, lips parted as she traces her bottom lip with her tongue.

"That's fucking right, little storm, you are mine. My own little hurricane."

It was cold but damn if I felt it right now, no, I was burning for her, my blood running so hot it was almost unbearable. I drop my hand from her neck, curling it around her hip to bring her further back from the tree, letting my other hand flick the button on her jeans and dive it inside, and beneath her panties.

She's fucking drenched, "What a mess you've made, princess, and all of this is for me."

"Rett, please," She rolls her hips against my hand as I slip a finger inside of her, pressing against her clit with the heel of my palm.

"Stay still baby," I order and when she obliges, I crouch, tugging at her pants until they're around her ankles. I remove one shoe and then the other before I take her jeans completely off, leaving her in just a white pair of lace panties. Turning her, I press her back against the tree, her jacket still done up. She breathes heavily, her cheeks bright with a mixture of the cold and her need. I tug the zipper down but leave the jacket on before I reach into my boot and pull out the hunting knife.

Her eyes widen, "What are you doing?"

"Shh, princess," I whisper, "Hold still.

Taking the neck of the sweater, I pull it away from her skin and place the edge of the blade to the material. The razor edge slices through the fabric as if it were nothing more than butter, and when the material parts, I take in the soft mounds of her breasts behind the white lace bra and trace my finger down the center of her stomach. Her muscles jump under the contact of my finger and when I look back up to her, desire burns so brightly in her eyes it almost flays me alive.

With the jacket and sweater hanging from her shoulders, I take the knife to the center of her bra, pulling it away from her skin before a quick tug slices it.

She cries out, the loudness of it startling the birds to take flight as my mouth latches onto one peaked nipple, sucking the hardened bud and teasing with my teeth.

With my tongue flicking lazily against her breast, I gently rub a finger against her pussy, above the material which is drenched thoroughly from her need for me. She would drive me damn crazy.

"Don't stop, please," She begs as I keep working her up, not that she needed much from me. She was so ready for me, but winding her up like this gave me so much satisfaction, there was no way I was stopping until she came for me like this.

Dropping to my knees, I push the panties to the side and grab the back of her knee, opening her up. She falls harder against the tree now that she's unbalanced, but I don't give her a chance, I bury myself into her cunt, tasting just how fucking hot she is for me.

Chuckling, I come away and look up at her, keeping my rhythm with a finger, "You want more, my little storm?"

"Please," she begs, pleading with her eyes for me to continue. She's so close, it wouldn't take much, "It aches, Rett. Make it stop."

"I'll always take care of you," I promise, thrusting two fingers into her. Her leg jerks over my shoulder and then tense when I bring my mouth back to her hot center, flicking my tongue on her swollen clit as my hand pumps into her body. Gripping my hair, she detonates against me, pussy clamping around my fingers as I continue to lick and suck her into my mouth.

"Too much," She gasps.

"Not enough," I argue.

I make quick work of my pants, tugging them down along with my boxers and do the same to her panties before I force her to turn again. I push her forward, making her bend as I line myself up with her, pussy still dripping, her inner thighs soaked.

I thrust hard, burying myself inside of her with a loud grunt. "Oh shit," She cries.

"So." Thrust. "Fucking." Thrust. "Good." My fingers bite into her flesh as I pound into her from behind, the sound of our skin slapping together obscenely loud in the quiet woods. She pushes back with every thrust of my hips, taking and giving, her flesh turning red from the punishing grip I have on her. She'll be wearing my finger marks on her pretty body, remembering how I owned her.

I fuck her hard, needing her to feel me, feel us, hammering into her so she knows there is only ever going to be us.

"I'm going to come," She whimpers, my cock sawing in and out of her body, covered in her wetness.

I groan, watching myself before the tell-tale zap of pleasure shoots down my spine. My hips turn jerky, slower as I wring the pleasure out of both of us, but I don't stand a chance when I feel her begin to contract around me, her pussy squeezing me like a vice.

I come so damn hard, stars burst behind my eyes. I empty myself inside of her, fingers holding her to me while I fill her up.

"God damn, princess," I kiss her spine before pulling out of her, watching as I leak from her cunt and down her inner thigh, "So fucking perfect and so fucking *mine*."

CHAPTER THIRTY-FOUR
everett

I get Arryn back to the cabin, she's cold, tired and hungry but that damn smile hasn't left her face.

Mine either.

Because damn, if I didn't want to do that again.

She cleans up in the bathroom while I get a fire started to heat this place back up and when she comes back out, I pile a shit ton of blankets on her to keep her warm until the flames can do the job.

I'm skirting around the issue now, though. We had to figure out a way of staging her death and making it as real as possible and I hated it. No matter how many distractions I allow myself, how many times I tell myself her death is not a reality, it fills me with so much dread, it cripples me.

Because that line is so very thin.

What if something goes wrong?

Claiming the job was already suspicious since I was working with her father only weeks before but to take Arryn too? I had to hope my reputation was enough to keep the questions away. I was brutal or so people believed, had no loyalty nor morals, which is exactly how I wanted people to see me.

No emotional connections, no ties, just a cold-hearted killer. It meant people couldn't use me. Couldn't use those I cared about against me.

My brothers were different since they were in the same profession, and no one was dumb enough to go after the best in the business, but I'd done a lot to make sure I didn't get attached to people.

Until Arryn.

And now I'm so irrevocably in love with her it physically pained me to have to pretend she was dead. And not only that, but it's also my name on the database that's going to claim the kill. My name. Her death was on me.

Regardless of the outcome we were aiming for, regardless that this was the best way to keep her safe and give her, her life back, I wasn't ashamed to admit it scared me.

Because what if I am not enough to protect her?

What if faking her death pushes us over that invisible line? What if this is tempting fate?

Swallowing down the bile that burns my throat, I prod the fire, moving the burning logs so I can get another piece inside. Embers burst from the logs, crackling loudly.

I understand Torin's grief now. Understand it in a way I couldn't before. When Grace died, and his son, I truly couldn't understand why it hit Torin as hard as it did. He was a shell of the man he used to be, the grief eating him up inside.

It made me entirely heartless to not try to understand it better, but we were raised to not have those kinds of weaknesses. The marriage was whatever, I assumed he wanted to continue our family legacy and was using Grace to do it. They got married and had a kid quick so it didn't occur to me that he could actually be in love.

I suppose having to do this now, with Arryn and the first person I have ever truly loved was the price I had to pay for the selfishness I used to think with.

I'd helped my brother with Maya because I saw what she meant to him, saw what she had done for him, how she had brought him back and knew my brother needed her. I never believed I'd be in the same boat as them now.

I glance towards Arryn who has dozed off on the couch, buried under a mountain of blankets, only the top of her head could be seen.

Tomorrow.

Tomorrow we would stage a scene and I'll upload the

images to the site. It would take a few hours before I would hear back on if the images were acceptable or not, but if I was going to do this, there was only one way it would end.

In success.

They will believe she's dead because it's me who did it.

I do not miss. I do not make mistakes.

For all they know, Arryn Lauder is no longer going to be a problem.

CHAPTER THIRTY-FIVE
arryn

Everett is quiet.

He moves through the cabin silently, brooding. His shoulders tense, spine stiff and face set in grim concentration. His laptop has remained open since we woke up this morning but he's yet to say a word. He's touched me gently, a quick caress of his fingers across my back, or a peck of his lips on my forehead, but no words.

It was making me edgy.

"You're making me nervous, Everett," I say to him. He's paced the room so much I was surprised he hadn't worn a hole into the floor.

"I'm trying to think," he says quietly, gently.

"About?" I press.

"My kills are almost always with a bullet. They're quick and effective."

"Effective? What does that even mean?"

"I aim for the skull, princess, and I don't miss."

"Oh."

He presses his lips together, "That isn't going to work for us. I don't have blood nor the skills to make it look realistic. I should have thought about this." He growls out that last bit more to himself.

"It's okay," I look around the room, "How much blood do you need?"

"The blood isn't just the problem, princess."

"You need to make it look like you shot me in the head, right? Does it matter if it's front or back?"

"Well, no," he frowns.

I nod, understanding, before I cross the room and pluck up his hunting knife. The blade glints in the light, the edge so damn sharp I doubt I'd have to really press hard for it to cut me. "So how much blood?"

"Put that down," he growls, storming towards me.

I move the knife away from him, "How much, Everett?"

"Put it down, Arryn," he demands, "you are not cutting yourself with that blade."

"We need blood, Everett, so if I have to cut myself then I will. I want this to be over."

"Give it to me." His tone broaches no arguments.

"Everett, please," I practically beg, "I need this to be over. We need to do this."

"Give it to me," he says.

Knowing there was no way I was winning or successfully doing it without him stopping me, I hand him the knife.

"Go lay down on the floor in front of the couch, on your front, facing away from the door."

My limbs tremble and my palms sweat as my heart picks up speed inside my chest. Everything screams that this is wrong, that I am in danger but inherently I know I am not. Blowing out a shaky breath, I get to my knees and then balance on my hands, subtly looking back to where Rett stands with the knife in one hand and the blade resting on his palm. He watches me carefully.

"Lay down."

I lay myself down gently, steadying my breath and turn my face towards the burning fire. Behind me I could hear him. He moves towards me and then sucks in a sharp, pained breath before the knife clatters to the floor.

It took a shit ton of strength not to move. Not to go to him. I knew what he had just done, and I wanted to make sure he was okay. I wanted to take care of him, clean him up but I couldn't. Not yet.

He stops behind me, and his hand suddenly pushes into my hair. I feel the wetness of his blood trickle down the back of my scalp as he mats up my hair, coating it in his blood. Once he's happy the back of my head is thoroughly coated in his blood, he moves his hand away, but he doesn't move.

With him so close, I can hear the drip of his blood as it flows from the wound he's inflicted on his hand. He's making a puddle behind my head and once he's done that, he moves around to the front of me. He's pale, his skin looking a little clammy like he's sick and there's so much blood covering his palm, dripping off the side and onto the floor.

He hovers his hand over my face, and I can't help but flinch when the first drop of warm blood lands on my cheek. He lets several more hit my skin before he takes his hand away and grabs a rag, wrapping it tightly around his palm. The edges of the rag are instantly soaked red, but he doesn't seem to notice. I lay as still as I can, not wanting to disturb the scene Rett has created. He works quietly and once his hand is thoroughly wrapped and he's satisfied, he moves to the fire and leans towards the edge, swiping his thumb there and gathering soot against his skin.

My brows pull down in confusion as he starts to rub it between his fingers, lightening the black color to more of a grey before he then starts to smudge it under my eyes.

His breath rushes out of him shakily.

"Keep your eyes open," he orders gently, "Stare towards the window, do not move, try to hold your breath."

I nod subtly.

"Good girl, it'll be over soon." He assures me, though I think it's also for himself.

He stands and steps away from me, and I listen to his careful footsteps as he crosses the room before he then comes back to me.

"Still, princess. Hold still."

I focus my eyes on the window, holding them open for as long as I can as Rett moves around above me. It feels like forever holding the same position, my heart pounding and begging for me to take a big breath instead of the slow, small ones I am taking. My eyes sting, the unforgiving floor bites into my cheekbone but still, I lay there, not moving. Lifeless. Dead.

Rett drops his phone onto the couch and then he's next to me, pulling me up from the floor, wiping his fingers over my cheeks, over the blood he put there, and his mouth is on mine. Desperate, full of need. I kiss him back; the metallic tang of blood is on my tongue, but I don't stop him.

"Shower," He rasps, "I need to get this blood off you."

He helps me from the floor and ushers me urgently towards the bathroom, getting the shower running.

"Calm down," I urge him as he rips at my clothes. "It's not real."

"I need to get it off you," He pleads.

"Okay," I still his shaking hands and take off my clothes for him, letting him guide me into the shower where he then joins me. There was nothing sexual about it, no heat or desire. His hands wash my hair twice, turning the water beneath my feet red. I could feel the rag catching in the strands but don't open my mouth and tell him to stop. I'll deal with him once he's calmed down. He needed to take care of me, and I'd let him.

When my hair is washed, he picks up the soap and squirts it into his uninjured palm before he then lifts it to my cheek, washing away the blood there and the soot under my eyes. He then does the rest of my body before his eyes lift to mine and his shoulders sag in defeat. I haul him to me, wrapping my arms around him and give him my strength. His heart pounds so hard I feel it against my own chest, can see the pulse point in his neck jumping wildly but still, I hold him. I run my fingers over the wet skin of his back, press my lips to his chest, I give him my warmth and my breath to bring him back to me.

And after a few long minutes, his arms finally lift and he embraces me back, hugging me tight to him.

"Too real," He rasps, "It looked too real."

"Then it will work, Rett," I assure him, "It'll all be over soon."

I feel him nod and after he's washed himself off, we

get dressed, heading back to the couch. I demand that he sits while I clean the blood from the floor, and then grab the small, and practically empty, first aid kit.

"I think this needs stitches," I wince at the long, straight gash on the palm of his hand, the skin on either side of the wound raw and red, the wound itself still steadily bleeding though not nearly as profusely as before.

"It'll be fine, princess."

I wasn't convinced and grab as much as I can from the box, but it wasn't a lot. It would be enough until we can get back to town and then I'll reassess it. There had to be a doctor here who could see to it, surely.

I place the gauze over the cut, pressing it down firmly and get him to hold it in place as I wrap a bandage around it tightly.

"Can I see them?" I ask when I'm satisfied with my work.

He looks down at the phone between us and unlocks the screen, the image before me so startling, I almost want to throw up.

CHAPTER THIRTY-SIX

everett

The image unsettles my stomach, making it hard not to throw up at the view of it.

It looks far too realistic, which in every sense was a good thing except looking at it made it all too real.

The hair at the back of Arryn's head is matted with my blood, a puddle sitting at the back of her head which has several strands floating in it. There was blood splattered on her pale cheek and the soot I'd placed under her eyes gave her a bruised lifeless look since her skin was so light. Her eyes stare lifelessly towards the window, the glow of the flame reflecting off her skin.

I'd captured several different angles, trying not to get too close to the area where the blood was at the back of her head since there is no bullet wound but it should be enough. These should be convincing enough.

"Are you sending them?" Arryn fidgets by my side.

"Yes," I nod as I close the images and get up from the couch to plug the phone into the laptop.

"They look real," she follows me into the kitchen and sits on the opposite side of the table, "How long will it take?"

"A few hours, they'll have the images checked for authenticity. I'll know if money is deposited."

"No money, no freedom," she whispers.

"Exactly that, princess."

"And what happens if no money is deposited?"

"I'll be listed as a hit."

She gasps, eyes widening, "You'll be a target!?" I don't have to give an answer for her to realize the truth.

"Everett!" She scolds. "Does Torin know this?"

"He does."

"And he just let you do it?"

"He didn't *let* me do anything. He knows I can handle it."

"We'll both be running forever, Rett," her eyes glisten, "If I knew…"

"It's going to work." I say the words, forcing myself to believe them.

Uploading the photos to the database, I mark the job as complete. I could spend the next few hours watching the screen, could torture us both with anxiety but I don't do that. I close the laptop and stare across the table towards my girl. She's picking at a dent in the table, worry creasing her face.

"I want to take you somewhere." I tell her, glancing towards the window where the sun still shines brilliantly. "Dress warm and wear your boots."

Arryn holds my hand with her gloved one, her breath coming out in white puffs in front of her face. As we step out of the shelter of the trees, the wind suddenly whips at our bodies, sending her hair flying around her face. The edge of the cliff looms ahead and that prickle of fear sends my hair to standing.

But Arryn feels no such thing. Her hand slips out of mine as her awe carries her forward, toward that cliff edge and the view beyond.

My feet stay planted right where they are. I wanted her to see it but that did not mean I had to go anywhere near that damn edge and the sheer drop. I could hear the sea crashing against the sharp rocks at the very bottom, listened to the shrill call of the birds as they battled the coastal wind that made the ocean below turbulent and unforgiving. Arryn goes worryingly close to the brink of the cliff, her hair blowing with the wind. The lighthouse sits directly across from us, the light off since the day was clear and beyond that, the town appeared more like Lego than a real town, the colors of the buildings a stark contrast to the greenery that surrounds it.

Boats bob like tiny little ants atop the water near the docks and I could even see Torin's house, the red blur outside, his truck. There was no way of making out if people were walking the streets or the docks, not this far up but it was serene. Peaceful. Just as long as I don't look down.

Arryn whips her head around to me, looking back over her shoulder with a smile that rivaled even the sun. She beams at me, everything about her reflecting the beauty that surrounds her.

"Come and look!" She calls over, turning back, "The water looks so surreal this high."

"I'm okay here, princess."

She turns back to me, "What?"

"Don't go too close to the edge." I tell her.

She cocks her head curiously, eyes assessing. "You're scared." A grin spreads on her face, "You're afraid of heights."

"No, I'm not, princess," I lie.

She turns to me fully then, her eyes alight with mischief and playfulness.

"Arryn," I warn, not liking where I think her mind is going. She takes a careful step back, rocks shifting under her weight. There was still a good ten feet between her and the edge of the cliff but unease swirls in my stomach.

"You're not scared, huh?" She teases, taking another step back. I take one forward.

"Princess, stop," I warn.

"Or what?" She cocks a brow and licks her teeth, "What are you going to do, my big scary assassin?"

"Come here and find out," I tell her, hoping to coax her to me.

"Or come here and tell me," She takes another step back, six feet now separating her from the edge. "You're afraid of heights, admit it." She says.

"Little storm," I practically beg.

Another step, and that gap between her and the edge was becoming precariously short, fraying my nerves. Fuck this.

I start towards her, and she takes two steps back, leaving her far too fucking close. A strong gust of wind will knock her right over that damn edge. I grip her and pull her back, putting space back between her and the edge.

She's laughing when I pull us to a stop, "It is not

funny, you would not survive that drop."

"Oh, I am aware," She kisses the edge of my mouth, "But I wouldn't have fallen."

"And how could you know that?" I growl, heart still pounding something furious inside my chest.

"Because you never would have allowed it."

"Don't do that again," I rasp against her cold lips, her breath warm against my own.

"You're afraid."

"Yes, little storm, I am afraid of heights."

"And I am afraid of the dark," she tells me on a whisper that is almost stolen by the howling wind, "There is no shame in admitting fear, Everett. Fear keeps us alive."

"Fear can also get you killed, princess."

"Fear makes you human," she argues.

"Fear makes you human," I agree, curling my finger beneath her chin to tilt her face to mine, "Please stay away from the edge."

"Yes, sir," She teases lightly, pressing her lips to mine, "It's so beautiful up here."

"I'm not sure it's the view that makes it beautiful," I say, "It's more the company."

"Charming as always."

CHAPTER THIRTY-SEVEN

everett

Amount of 500,000 (five hundred thousand) US Dollars deposited to Everett Walker Avery by Farrow Industries.

"Five hundred thousand," Arryn blows out a breath, "Damn I'm expensive."

The sickness that had churned the moment I noticed the notification on the laptop, dissipates when I look up and notice the amusement on Arryn's face. This should be morbid and sickening and yet she found it fucking funny.

"What do you want to do with it?" I ask.

"The money?"

I nod, picking up her hand that was resting on the tabletop, running my fingers down each one of hers.

"Charity?" She says, "I'd like to donate it."

"Just pick one or several, I'll sort the rest." I explain.

"So now we plan our epic come back, right?" Her eyes twinkle, "We can go back."

"I'll watch for the Ware's," I tell her, "When they show themselves, we can make our move. Without them we can't go back. We need to move quick to end them both before they catch wind that you're still alive."

"How are you going to know?"

"I have my ways, princess," I kiss the center of her palm, "Don't worry about that."

"So, what now?"

"We can continue as we are, we are safe here for now. Snow is coming though; we'll be better off in the town."

We make it to Torin's house by the time the sun sets and clouds have rolled in from the ocean, bringing with it icy winds and the promise of more snow. Everything was calm, despite the turbulent sea that was determined to batter this tiny island, everything had gone to plan. They had believed those images, believed Arryn was dead somewhere, shot in the back of the head and left to rot. They didn't much care what happened to the body after the job was complete, some add extra instructions, like requiring clean up or making it look like an accident but there was just one instruction and that was to kill her and leave her.

I was glad for it since most extras required extra proof, like a hole in the ground, the body wrapped in tarp and thrown inside and I think if we had had to go to those lengths I would have likely gone mad.

But my bank was sitting five hundred thousand dollars heavier until I could make the deposits to charity like Arryn had asked.

We're laying in bed later that night when Arryn turns to me, the soft light being emitted from the lamp kissing the side of her face, "Farrow Industries." She says quietly.

"What about them?"

"That's who made the payment."

"Yes," I nod, "My father worked for them before Torin, and I were born and continued to until he died. He trained us for them."

"It just seems so normal."

"The Farrow's use businesses to hide the money made through their hit list. From huge corporations to tiny little cafes and hotels. They siphon money into each one and place it in the banks of each business which are all then overlooked by Farrow Industries. Payments for jobs always come through them. They take a cut from every contract."

"How big are they?"

"Honestly, I do not truly know. No one knows the family who runs it. They're simply known as Farrow. It could be one man; it could be twenty. They remain anonymous, likely to protect their own asses since they're greedy, selfish assholes and always have been."

"You've worked for them your whole life," she points out.

"I've never known anything else. They made me money, and money was all I wanted, to begin with, that and a legacy separate to my brothers and father. But if you piss off the Farrow's you'll know about it. No one has successfully left their ranks without ending up dead."

"Torin?"

"He was the first. He was a favorite though so perhaps they gave him his freedom since he made them so much money."

"They sound like awful people."

"When you're born in darkness, nothing is impossible. The world is greedy and corrupt, and death is spilled far more often than one realizes."

"Torin," Arryn continues, "Did he know his retirement could have gotten him killed?"

"Yes," I confirm, tucking her hair behind her ear, "But he was willing to risk it for Grace and his son. I think the Farrow's were sure he'd be back, and he was… but that had consequences. Tragic ones."

"What happened?"

With a long, heavy sigh I answer, "His wife, the one he left the organization for, died, along with their infant son."

Color drains from her face, "They killed them?"

"No, I think it would have been easier if they had. They died in a storm. Torin and I went to the mainland for a job, he'd already retired at this point, but I'd convinced him to do one last job with me. We worked together often, and I wanted my brother. He had agreed. We did the job and got paid.

"I stayed on the mainland after it was done, and Torin got on that boat with his wife and son. Torin made it back but they didn't. He blamed himself for it. For a long time, my brother was wasting away here on this island, five years he didn't speak to anyone, see anyone, do much of anything really until Maya and Harper."

She shifts closer, her hand sliding across my chest, "If they find out…"

"They're not going to find out. Now that the payment has been made, no one will ever look at it again. To them you're dead and it's done. If they were going to figure it out, they would have when I sent the photos."

"And what about when you go after the Ware's?"

"They're not part of the organization, their deaths

won't even be noticed."

"So, you have everything figured out?"

"To keep you safe," I tell her, "I'll burn the fucking world."

"And they say romance is dead," she laughs loudly, "I don't need any world burning, Everett. Just my life back. Our life."

"I'll give you the very best."

CHAPTER THIRTY-EIGHT
arryn

We'd been staying with Torin and Maya for days now, snow has come down thick and heavy, covering the town in white blankets that were almost impossible to walk through. There were no snowplows here, just shovels and sheer willpower to keep the town going.

And it worked. Everyone worked to clear the streets as best as possible, everyone chipped in to chop firewood, shovel snow and deliver essentials to the ones who needed the help most. School was cancelled for Harper which meant I got to spend a couple days just hanging out with the little lady. And I loved every minute of it. She was such a sweet little girl, incredibly smart and unnervingly observant. She saw everything, even the stuff you desperately wanted to hide.

Everett was helping Torin with the needs of the town; Maya was helping Ruthie down at the lodge and I'd offered to keep an eye on Harper while they did all that.

She was currently sitting on the bed Rett and I were sharing, swinging her legs off the side while I unpacked the bags we had neglected to do since we weren't sure how long we were staying for.

It seemed we weren't going anywhere for a while, and I was sick of living out of duffels and suitcases.

"I was never allowed to play in the snow!" Harper says as I place one of Rett's sweaters on a hanger, "momma and I built our first snowman the other day. Daddy helped."

My heart warms at hearing her call Torin daddy, Maya and Harper deserved so much happiness and from what Rett told me about his brother, Torin deserved it too.

I reach into the bag, "What did you call your snowman?" I ask as I pull out a small bag where the contents rattle a little inside.

"Kevin." Harper answers so nonchalantly, so easily that I'm shocked for a moment.

"Kevin!?" I laugh, looking back to the small girl on the bed.

Harper grins back at me, her round, rosy cheeks lifting with the full expression, eyes beaming, "He had a carrot nose. Do you want to build one with me!?"

"I would love to!" I laugh, turning back to the small bag in hand, "We'll do it after I've put away the rest of these things."

I open the zip on the bag, trying to figure out where to put it and stop short.

There are three syringes inside, all filled with a clear liquid, and it doesn't take me long to realize what they are.

Rett sedated me on the boat when we first arrived and looking at the slip of paper stuffed in with them, these were backups. Putting the syringe subtly back inside the bag, I zip it up and carefully stash it in the drawer by the side of the bed I sleep on. I didn't want them just lying around nor did I want them accessible. I lock the drawer and stash the key in a shoe at the back of the wardrobe, before I turn all my attention to the small girl waiting to build a snowman with me. We head out into the snow, the cold already sinking beneath my skin.

Harper's all wrapped up in a puffer coat with a hat that almost covers her eyes and mittens and she's started rolling a ball in the snow, pushing it around and around to try build it up. She has a pile of old winter accessories laying at the foot of the porch steps and a lonely carrot buried beneath it all.

"We will call him Phil," Harper huffs, pushing all her weight into the ball but it wasn't going anywhere. So, she stops and starts building on top of it, mushing snow into the sides to build up the snowman base.

"Phil the snowman, I like it."

I get to my knees to help, pushing snow into the base and eventually we have a good solid foundation. I start on the second section when my collar is suddenly yanked, and ice is thrown down my back.

I let out a shocked scream, biting my tongue so I don't curse as the snow gets everywhere under my layers, chilling me before it melts and leaves me wet. I spin to find Everett with a shit eating grin on his face, biting his lip as if to stop from laughing.

"I am going to murder you!" I yell at him, lunging for him as I scoop up a handful of snow. But I should have guessed catching him would be impossible. The man was a skilled hunter, there was no way he would easily become the prey. I launch my snowball at him, aiming for his head but miss.

He chuckles and Harper squeals, diving for cover behind the half-built snowman. "Everett!" I squeal as he throws his own back. I don't dodge it in time, and it hits me square in the back.

"Come on, princess," He taunts, "Where's that drive to kill me gone?"

"You want drive?" I growl, making the perfect round snowy projectile while also hiding behind the porch, "I'll give you drive, Everett Avery."

"Oh, I love it when you get feisty, little storm," he licks his lips, "Win and I might even let you have a little control."

He didn't have to say much more than that for me to know what he meant. I wasn't sure what it would be like if *I* had the control, how it would end but hey, I was curious. And a sore loser.

I keep low as I round the porch, "There she is," his eyes flare, "My pretty little princess."

I duck and sprint to where Harper is, "We're a team," I tell her, "You go left, I go right."

She grins, "Uncle Rett is old, he can't keep up with me." She gloats.

"I heard that!" Rett hollers, feigning offence. "Using children is immoral, little storm, shame on you."

"All is fair in love and war, Everett," I taunt, darting out when Harper does. She launches her snowball and hits Rett on the shoulder and I throw mine, hitting him right in the chest. We both cheer at our victory.

"I've been shot!" Rett gasps dramatically, dropping to his knees, "The war is over!"

Harper laughs as she runs over to him and something warm and bubbly twists in my stomach as I watch him catch her, laughing with her as he smooshes snow into the top of her hat.

Rett would make a great father, he's protective and loves so damn fiercely.

We dust off the snow at the door and head in. I was wet and shivering so I head upstairs to change, listening to the giggles from Harper and Rett's deep chuckle as I climb the stairs.

I'm stripping before I've even stepped foot into the room, wanting to get the cold water off my skin and dry but something on the bed catches my attention.

It wasn't there when I went out with Harper, and I wasn't sure Rett had come inside before he'd initiated that snowball fight.

Skeptical, but curious, I head towards it. On top of the brown envelope is a phone, the screen dark.

I pick it up and hit the button on the side to unlock the screen but it remains blank so pick up the envelope instead. It's sealed but it's thick and has no name on the front to tell me who it is addressed to. Sliding my finger under a gap at the flap, I tear it open and pull out what appears to be glossy photopaper.

Turning them around in my hands I feel my breath get stuck in my throat, my blood turning thick and cold.

Familiar eyes stare back at me, so dark in color they almost looked black, framed by thick lashes but where they're usually so full of life and light, here they look dull, shadowed in blue and purple that tells of her exhaustion. There were no physical marks I could see but not all trauma leaves scars.

At her side is a man I recognize all too easily.

Malakai Ware stands at my sister's side, a threat if I ever did see one.

There are more photos, so I lay the one of my sister down and shuffle through the others.

My death. Or my fictional one at least, and on each one I see three words scrawled across them all…

You or her...

They had my sister.

They knew I was alive. Where I was.

And they were using the one thing sure to bring me to them.

Olivia.

I get to the last picture and this one isn't me, it's another photo of my sister, in this one she is crying at my father's funeral, dressed in black, her skin pale and worn.

It was a threat, a lesson that taught me they'd always known where she was, always had access to her and only now they were acting on it because of what I did. Because of what Rett and I tried to lie about.

A sob chokes me, my limbs aching with such heavy grief even holding up these pictures physically pained me. My arm drops and all of the photos slip from my fingers, and as if on command the screen on the phone lights up with a message.

I reach for it, swallowing down the scream I want to unleash.

And even though they're words on a screen, the weight they carry has my knees buckling. They have my throat closing.

Arryn Lauder.

Death marked.

Olivia Lauder.

Death marked.

Everett Avery.

Death marked.

Torin Avery

Death marked.

Maya Avery

Death marked.

My sob comes out on a whimper as I read Harper's name, and then Ruthie's and then Vanessa's. And so, it goes. Over and over. Naming every person I have had contact with, every person I care about.

Someone had got into the house without anyone knowing, had planted this here. They had easy access to us, and this threat just proved it.

The phone buzzes in my hand and a new message appears on the screen.

And I know how to make all of this end.

And it means returning to the mainland, returning to my hotel and my sister.

This isn't going away, there is no escape, not without tragic consequences and my life is not worth all of theirs.

CHAPTER THIRTY-NINE
arryn

My hand aches with how hard I am clenching it, my heart thumping wildly inside my chest. The house is quiet, dark, the night clear outside the window.

I can hear Everett in the bathroom, he'd been in there for ten minutes and I'd used the free time to get prepared. I hated that I was doing this, that what I was about to do to him was going to be the last thing he remembered of me.

I place the letter I wrote in the envelope and slide it under my pillow just in time for him to come out of the bathroom, a towel around his trim hips, water sluicing down his hard muscles. He grins at me, completely unaware and sits on the side of the bed.

Crawling over to him, the item in my hand hidden, I

wrap my arms around his neck. He smiles even wider when I climb onto his lap, letting my lips find his. I kiss him deeply, expressing everything I haven't been able to say. I kiss him like the world is ending because while it won't for him, it will for me.

And he kisses me back just as vehemently, his tongue sliding against mine, his hands in my hair, tangling up the strands in his strong fingers. And then I pop the cap, holding him close as I lift and stab it into his neck.

He goes still beneath me as I compress the plunger and the sedative disappears into his system.

"Arryn," he rasps, his words slurring.

"I'm sorry, I'm so fucking sorry, Everett," I whisper, tears slipping down my cheeks as I help to lay him down on the mattress, "I didn't have a choice and you wouldn't have let me go."

"Pr – pr – princess," My heart is breaking, cracking into thousands of little pieces as a single tear slips out of the side of Rett's eye, disappearing into the thick hair at the side of his head.

"I love you, Everett Avery." I declare, "Thank you for being the one to show me it was real."

"Don't," his words are coming slower, quieter, weakening as the sedative takes hold fully, "Go. Don't go."

"Goodbye Everett."

His eyes close and his body goes limp.

I didn't know how long the sedative would keep him out for, long enough I suspected for me to get to the boat that was waiting for me on the docks. I take the envelope out from under the pillow and place it on top so he'll see it when he wakes and can understand why I did this. I didn't want him to hate me. I needed him to know that he owns my heart.

Glancing at the time on the phone that was delivered earlier, I notice I still have ten minutes before I needed to be at the docks.

The text earlier had given me instructions on how to end the threats against everyone I cared about. I was told to leave here, alone. Failure to do that would result in one person dying, likely Olivia since she's the one he had in reach. They explained there would be a boat waiting at half past midnight and the man would then take me to my sister and Malakai.

I knew I wasn't going to see another sunrise and I wished I'd spent more time watching it, with Rett and Harper, and Maya and Torin. I wished I'd had that girl's night Vanessa was trying to arrange with me, wished I'd helped Ruthie bake those cookies. I wished I had longer to say goodbye to my little sister, I doubted I'd even be able to hold her one last time.

I hadn't thought about my own death but now, as I place my feet into the boots Rett bought me and slide my arms into the jacket, I realize I am fucking terrified to die.

My hands are shaking as I creep through the dark and quiet house, everyone sleeping and dreaming while I was living a nightmare.

I hoped they wouldn't hate me after this but if they did, I could understand that.

I slip out into the night silently, the cold biting at my skin and trying to chase me back inside. But I wouldn't be selfish about this, I wouldn't put anyone's life at risk.

The snow crunches under my feet as I walk through it, and the short distance towards the dock.

There's a boat waiting, bobbing on the dark, inky water, a single light shining on the silhouette of a large man. I couldn't make out any details other than the fact that he was huge, taller than Everett and Torin and he stands so still it was like I was staring at a statue.

"Arryn Lauder?" His voice, a deep smoky timbre sends alarms ringing in my head. My knees are shaking, my heart pounding so hard it feels like it's trying to escape through my ribs.

"Yes," I answer, my voice almost swallowed by the sound of the sea.

"Get in."

Shakily, I climb into the boat and instantly fall onto the bench, my knees unable to hold me up any longer. He doesn't waste any time in getting us moving and doesn't say a single word to me as he takes us away from the dock and out further into the bay. I look back at the dark house, staring at it as if wishing one of the lights would turn on. Someone would see me going but they don't. The house gets smaller and smaller, until I can no longer see it in the darkness, and I leave it behind. Leave *him* behind.

Thirty minutes pass slowly, the sound of the boat and waves almost deafening but I finally look to the man driving, his broad back to me. I can see his hair is longer, tied up with wispy strands whipping around with the wind but that's as much detail about him that I can gather.

"What is your name?" I ask.

His chin tilts slightly as if looking over his shoulder, "Does it change the outcome?" He retorts.

"No, but if you're the last person I'm going to see…" I trail off, "Never mind."

"My brothers should have known better than to play the system."

My eyes widen and I practically break my own damn neck as I whip around to stare at him, "Your brothers!?" I gasp, "You're Kolten!"

He doesn't speak again as he ferries me back to the mainland.

When we're there, he anchors up and even helps me out of the boat with a gentle hand but then he ushers me into a car.

"Will you do it?" I ask from the backseat.

"Malakai has requested for you not to be harmed," He explains.

"You work for him?"

"I work for myself," he growls.

"If Everett finds out about this," I whisper, "He'll never forgive you."

I see Kolten stiffen in the passing city lights.

"Don't let him find out," I say to him, "Don't tell him."

"I will handle my brother."

"Don't let them hurt him," I beg, "Please, Kolten."

I didn't know why I was begging this man, the same man delivering me to my death but instinctively I knew he would ensure Everett would stay safe. He may be doing this to me, but they're his brothers.

"It'll be over soon," Kolten says quietly.

Tears slip down my cheeks as I fall quiet, sagging into the plush leather seat as I watch the city pass me by in a blur of bright light.

My fear ramps up several notches as the Lauder Hotel comes into view, the light from the crystal chandelier spilling out into the road in front of it. There was no one waiting outside for us, no guests lingering on the steps smoking cigarettes, no drunken men stumbling in from a night at a casino. It is deathly quiet. Eerily empty.

No one around to witness my comeback or my death.

Kolten pulls the car to a stop out front and gets out, opening my door for me but fear keeps me rooted to the spot.

This was it.

The end.

CHAPTER FORTY

I'm so sorry Everett.

I am so fucking sorry.

I didn't get to say goodbye or tell you that I love you. I knew you wouldn't let me go if you knew the truth and a part of me loves you for that, but I couldn't be selfish in this. I couldn't put you and your family at risk.

They have my sister, you'll see everything in this envelope, so I really hope you can understand why I had to do this.

By the time you wake up, I'll probably be gone. If they let you, take my body. Don't let them bury me in some nameless grave.

These past few weeks have been incredible for me. You have made me come alive and experience life in a completely new way. I am so grateful to you for that.

I know I gave you shit, I know I was difficult, but you didn't let that stop you from showing me what love is.

You were right all along, the love I read in books is real. You were my fairytale.

If this had ended differently, I would have stayed with you in Ravenpeak, we would have lived in that cozy little cabin during the summer and figure something out for the winter. We would have had babies. Lots of babies. I would have liked to be a mother and you would have been the best dad. I know it.

When this is done, I'd like to be cremated. I don't want to be buried where I'll rot and be forgotten.

Scatter my ashes off the cliff where you told me of your fear of heights. I know you won't like it but for me, please. I want the wind to take me away and the ocean to claim me.

I'm sorry this is the way it ends.

Know I love you.

Thank you for being my fairytale.

Forever yours

Arryn

CHAPTER FORTY-ONE
arryn

Kolten walks behind me, our steps echoing through the empty foyer. No staff, no guests, just us and our loud steps on the marble floor. Quiet classical music plays through the speakers hidden throughout the hotel, a soft melody that we often choose for its elegance and serenity.

It sounds more ominous now than peaceful. The notes whip through my body, getting faster and faster as if to match the speed of my heart.

A guiding hand on the small of my back turns me into the dining room, the restaurant still set up as if to take guests. Candles are lit on the tables, jugs of water in the center with single roses set in tall thin vases. The lights are dimmed and the fire burning bright in the hearth at the end of the long room. All curtains are drawn and sitting in front of the fire is Malakai Ware, his father, and my sister.

She looks unharmed, but her skin is pale, and tears run steadily over her cheeks, her mascara leaving tracks.

"Olivia!" I start to run but a quick hand on my arm stops my forward motion so suddenly I fall back.

I hear her sob break, a wail so devastating it ruins me and whatever I had left of my heart shatters some more.

Kenneth stands and sneers at me, his face twisted into complete and utter hatred while his son remains sat and calm, his ankle resting on his knee, fingers steepled beneath his chin.

Kolt brings me to a stop about ten feet away from them. I scan Olivia more thoroughly now that I was closer. There were no obvious injuries even if the shadows beneath her eyes look like deep bruises over exhaustion. She has no color in her skin, even her mouth and her eyes are dull.

"I'm so sorry," I whisper to her, her eyes filling with fresh tears. "It wasn't supposed to end this way."

"And just what way was it supposed to end, Miss Lauder?" Malakai speaks, his cruel mouth tipping up slightly as if he knows how I will answer.

He's a beautiful man just like the devil once was. And the way he smiles at me, with such cruelty, I wonder if he's been sent straight from hell.

"With you dead," I growl honestly.

He chuckles, "Not a great end for me."

"A fitting end," I snap.

Malakai casts his eyes behind me, and I feel Kolten step up, his presence like a looming shadow. "Your debt is paid, Kolten. You are free to leave."

"Sir," Kolten responds gruffly and takes a step back, "I will stay to see this through."

"Very well," Malakai nods and stands, bringing with him my sister who snatches out of his grip.

"I see both the Lauder girls like to put up a bit of a fight," he snatches a long strand of Olivia's hair, "I suppose you understand how this will end."

"She goes free?" I ask.

"That was the deal. You for her."

"She knows too much, Malakai, kill them both. End the Lauder line once and for all." Kenneth spits, stepping towards my sister.

I lunge between them. Now that Kolten wasn't as close, I was able to and Kenneth stumbles back, eyes widening. I go straight for the fire tools, grabbing the fire poker and hold it out in front of me, my back to Olivia and Malakai.

The latter man laughs again, as if this is the funniest thing in the world.

"Arryn, stop," Olivia pleads, "You have to go. Let

them have me."

"I don't think so," Malakai says, "Olivia darling, your sister belongs to me."

"Take me instead!" Olivia begs.

"No!" My shock at Olivia's words leaves me exposed and Kenneth grabs the poker, ripping it from my grip.

I hear it as he whips it up and brace for a hit.

"Stop!" Malakai orders abruptly and before the poker can hit me, Kolten snatches out an arm and grabs it.

I use the distraction to grab Olivia, pulling her to me and stepping out of the way. She latches her arms around me, burying her face into my neck.

"I can't do this," She cries, "I can't do this again."

"Shh," I stroke her hair, feeling how thin she's become in the past few weeks.

"I can't watch you die, Arryn, I can't do it again."

"It's going to be okay," I whisper, staring over her shoulder at Malakai who is speaking with Kenneth. They were so confident we weren't going to fight that none of them were looking at us. Kenneth is arguing quietly with his son, and I cast my eyes to Kolten. He is watching.

Keen eyes analyze us. Kolten is very different to both his brothers, and then I remember Rett telling me he was adopted.

Tall, broad, and so fucking big he towers over every

man in this room, with long dark hair he has pulled up and out of his face. Tan with dark eyes framed by thick lashes and thick scruff that surrounds his mouth. He's handsome but stern, a hardness to him that neither brother has. I could not read him, not even a little.

Olivia cries against me, completely broken and I knew whatever happened to me next, she wouldn't survive it.

Slowly, I take us both to the floor and I bring her into my lap, just like I used to do when we were children, and she had a nightmare. Before all the death and the blood and terror. I hold her like she was the same little girl. I stroke her hair and rock her back and forth, as if I wasn't about to die, as if the men in the room with us weren't ruthless killers.

"Don't leave me again," she begs.

"I'm sorry," I whisper, "I'm so, so sorry. But I have to go."

"No." she says, over and over, just that one simple two letter word.

"Get up," I hear Malakai say, whatever argument he was having with his father clearly over now.

I look up at the man who helped kill my father and was about to do the same to me, "Please, if there is a heart in your chest, don't make her watch."

"It appears I have another idea, Miss Lauder," is all he says back. Kenneth seems as shocked as me if his sputtering and half finished sentences were anything to go by.

My brows draw down, "What?"

But I don't get an answer when all hell breaks loose in a riot of gunfire and glass shattering.

CHAPTER FORTY-TWO
everett

The letter is a ball in my hand as the boat speeds across the water, the icy wind battering my body, so cold I'm numb but I didn't have spare thought to think about the pain it was causing. Not when my heart was being ripped from my chest as I recall each word in Arryn's letter.

She wasn't leaving me.

She was not leaving like this.

Torin drives as fast as the boat will allow and I called in a favor with one of my contacts, so knew someone was going to be at the docks when we arrived. I was still feeling lethargic from the sedative, but the dose wasn't high, it'll wear off soon enough and with the adrenaline pumping furiously through me, the effects of the drug barely register.

But fear was making it hard to breathe.

What if I was too late?

We make it to the mainland and as planned, the car was waiting for us. My guy throws me the keys, but I don't have time for talking now. My girl needs me.

She fucking needs me.

Torin gets in the passenger seat and the door hasn't even closed when I floor the pedal and the tires spin on the wet and icy tarmac. The city flies by in a blur of color and noise, but I can't see anything other than those words on the paper.

You are my fairytale.

It was going to be happily ever after too. Fuck. Fairytales don't end this way.

"Slow down, Rett," Torin growls, "If you want to make it there in one damn piece."

"I can't," I choke.

"We're going to make it, brother," Torin says gently.

But I'm not so sure.

I fucked up. Malakai and Kenneth Ware were clever, they outsmarted me, and right now they've won.

The death marks, the threats, they had more power than I could have ever realized, and I was starting to believe they weren't who they said they were.

The Lauder Hotel sits like a shining beacon ahead, brightly lit when everything around is so dark. I slam on the brakes, the car squealing across the tarmac as it comes to a stop right in front of the door. My feet hit the concrete but before I can slam through the doors, Torin pulls me back.

"Remember who the fuck you are, Everett," He orders, "You'll get yourself killed."

"She's in there."

"And so are they!"

My breath whooshes from me and I look around, noticing how empty it is. There is not a single other person, no guests, or staff. The foyer is a ghost town, the roads around the hotel completely barren.

Inhaling a calming breath, I shut out the noise, drown out the distraction and turn to face the foyer.

When we know it's clear we both head inside, silent, invisible.

And then I hear her voice, just a sweet murmur, a whisper of sound but I would recognize her in any room, at anytime, anywhere.

She is mine.

I see her on the floor in front of the fire.

"Kolten," Torin growls. I spot our estranged brother standing close to where Malakai and Kenneth are speaking. He doesn't say anything, but he watches my girl and her sister.

The betrayal rips open new wounds, but I had a task to handle before I dealt with my brother.

"Get up," Malakai says.

Arryn stares up at him, "Please, if there's a heart in your chest, don't make her watch."

"It appears I have another idea, Miss Lauder." Malakai answers cryptically.

I use the fact that they're distracted to my advantage.

With a nod at Torin, we raise our weapons and storm the room.

There are three people in this room that I need to stay alive, the other two I'm going to bury so far into the ground, no one will ever find them. They'll be nothing more than the dirt under my shoes.

The door slams open and with an aim so accurate, I fire three times. Two of them were warning shots that shatter glass, the third hitting Kenneth between the eyes. His blood splatters up the wall above the fire but my shot on Malakai is blocked by Kolten stepping in front of him.

Silence falls and heavy breathing fills the space.

"Well, that was quite the entrance," Malakai steps out from behind my brother and I level the gun, ready to take the shot.

"Kolten, be sure to remind your brother what happens

if I die at his hand."

Kolten pleads with his eyes, imploring so much emotion into his expression it catches me off guard for a moment. Kolten doesn't show emotion.

"Death. To your murderer and his entire family."

"Oh, of course," Malakai, seemingly more confident now he knew I could do nothing here, steps towards me, "You don't know who I am, Everett."

My eyes latch onto Arryn as he continues speaking.

"My name is Malakai Farrow."

"Fuck," Torin growls. But I'm still staring at Arryn, his words taking a moment to register. Farrow. *Farrow Industries.*

"This is all rather messy, isn't it," Malakai tuts, staring down at Kenneth, "You went and ruined my cover."

"Farrow?" Arryn repeats the name and I subtly nod at her. Farrow of Farrow industries and the man behind the organization. Each Farrow takes on from the last but they each become more brutal, more powerful. Malakai's father was in charge when I first started working for them and after his death, his son. Never named but a presence always there. We only get the bare minimum in information about them, just news when someone new takes over from the last.

Powerful. Deadly. Undefeatable.

"Why don't we all take a seat?" Malakai walks casually to the bar and plucks a bottle of Macallan from the shelf, "If we're going to come to some sort of arrangement, it will require some drinks."

He whistles a tune as he strolls to the high back chairs situated around an oak round table, the candle burning in the center.

"Put the guns away, gentlemen, no one else needs to die tonight. Not yet at least."

My hand is holding my own weapon so tightly my muscles have cramped and my fingers ache with the tightness.

"Go ahead and kill me, Everett," Malakai looks me right in the eye, "Death doesn't scare me."

"You die and they all die," I growl.

"It is the way." He glances towards Arryn, "Go to your woman, Everett and then sit down. My patience is wearing thin."

"Rett," My name comes out on a broken cry, and I snap out of whatever was holding me in place and cross the space between us in large, sure steps. In the next second, I have her in my arms and she's clinging to me.

"I'm sorry," she whimpers, over and over, "I'm sorry."

"I've got you," I vow, "I'm here princess."

"I don't want to die," she whispers.

"We need to sit, princess," I explain to her, "Or none of us will be leaving this hotel."

CHAPTER FORTY-THREE
everett

Malakai Farrow sits opposite me. The man I have been working for, for countless years, the ruthless, brutal man that takes no prisoners and shows no mercy.

He was the one targeting Arryn.

It doesn't change anything. I wouldn't have changed a single thing even if I had known. But now I can't kill him. I can't end this.

Kenneth's body lays still and bleeding in front of the fire, his head split open and leaking all over the floor.

Arryn is at my side, her whole-body trembling while Olivia sits deathly still at her side. Kolt and Torin frame Malakai, the latter brother seething quietly in his chair. I'd pulled him into this. There was a chance none of us left here tonight and Maya would be left alone with Harper and her unborn baby.

I wasn't stupid enough to believe Malakai was here without backup and protection. It would be several of his best men, the best killers all charged with keeping him safe, and should something happen to the man himself, it'll be them who follow through with the order to take out his killer and their entire family.

Both Torin and I had been offered spots on that table, but both had declined. We wanted the freedom that came with choosing our targets.

Kolt hadn't had such thoughts.

Malakai pours the Macallan into the crystal glasses in front of each of us, no one saying a word.

Beneath the table, I take Arryn's hand, delicately stroking my thumb over her knuckles to try and soothe her.

"You Avery's are something else," Malakai begins, "First I lose one of my best killers," he pointedly looks at Torin, "Then his brother fakes my targets death and kills the man I was using for cover."

"Kenneth wasn't your father," Torin says.

"Fuck no," Malakai scoffs, "He was just the man I was using while I handled some business. I needed something from him, and he needed something from me, it was a transactional relationship."

"What business?"

"That's where you all come in," Malakai grins, whatever plan he has in place involves all of us somehow and I had a feeling it wasn't going to be easy. "I will release you all. Kolten has served his debt, he is free to go, Torin too, but you, Everett, and your darling woman have a price to pay."

"P-please," Olivia speaks for the first time since we got here, "Don't hurt my sister."

Malakai flicks his eyes to the girl, letting them scan her slowly, "Well it all depends on the answer to my next statement."

"Which is?" Arryn snaps, impatient and seething. She's tense, ready to lunge should she need to.

"I need a wife."

"No." I growl.

"While Arryn is very pretty, Everett, she is not who I have in mind."

"Me?" Olivia squeaks.

"Yes, Miss Lauder."

"Why!?" I growl, "you can't need her status or money."

"Because Everett, all Farrow's are expected to marry within six years of taking the business. I was planning a wedding to Kenneth's niece, but I don't like her much. She's like her uncle, greedy and spoiled and since I no longer have any ties to keep me bound to that deal," He flicks his eyes to Kenneth's cooling body.

"Little Olivia here is the perfect candidate. A strong background and status and quite frankly, I like little broken things." Those last words are aimed directly at the youngest Lauder.

"And if we don't agree?" Arryn grits her teeth.

"Then the death marks stay in place. I have men ready to go at a push of a button. I can assure you, you won't win against them."

Arryn stands abruptly, ready to fight but Olivia speaks first. "I'll do it."

"Olivia!" Arryn gasps.

"Arranged marriages happen all the time," Olivia speaks softly, "in our circles, it's not uncommon."

"You do know who he is!?" Arryn pleads, stepping towards her sister.

I grip her wrist, keeping her from flying off at Malakai. She's brimming with enough anger that rational and logical thought aren't keeping her controlled right now.

"The devil," Olivia says, "But there's been too much death."

"Very good," Malakai grins, pulling out a folded piece of paper from the inside of his suit pocket, "I had this drawn up, an agreement of sorts. Sign here, please Miss Lauder."

He slides the paper towards Olivia with a pen.

"Don't," Arryn begs but her youngest sister steels her spine and picks up the pen.

"Please, Oli," Arryn cries, "Don't sign it!"

The scratch of the nib on the paper is loud, like the chiming of a death bell. Olivia had sealed her fate to save her sister.

"There was nothing you could have done," Olivia says to Arryn some few hours later, the sisters curled up on the couch in a room we picked to stay in for the night, "I'll figure out a way of getting out of it."

Arryn shakes her head, "This was not your burden to bear."

"And it was yours?" Olivia scoffs. "It's always been your burden, it's my turn to save you."

Torin paces on the phone near the window, the conversation with Maya being taken in hushed tones.

We would go back to the mainland in the morning but right now we all needed some sleep. Kolten hangs back by the door, ever silent, ever watching and my anger for him was still boiling at the surface.

"He's dangerous," I tell Olivia, "You have to be incredibly careful around him."

"I plan on making his life hell," Olivia growls, "I don't have the power like he does but trust me, I can make him wish I never signed that piece of paper."

"When will he contact her for the wedding?" Arryn asks me, her eyes rimmed red and puffy from tears.

"Could be weeks or days, he's unpredictable."

"He'll let us see her, right?" Arryn gasps, panic filling her voice.

"I don't know, little storm."

I turn my attention to my adopted brother, teeth gritting even just looking at him, "You took her from me." I accuse.

"I had orders." Kolt replies casually.

"I'm your fucking brother!"

"So is Torin. I had no choice."

"What do you mean you had no fucking choice!?" I growl, stepping up to my brother. He'd kill me easily but at this point I didn't fucking care.

"I had a debt to pay."

"What did you owe him."

"A life."

"Who's life!?" I shove his shoulder, "Who did you choose over me!?"

"It wasn't a choice I ever expected to have to make, Everett," He yells at me, "You knew better!"

"And I would have done it again!" We're nose to

nose now, my chest heaving with my ire, blood boiling and fingers twitching to hit him, "We took you in. We are your brothers. You betrayed me!"

"I took Torin's price," Kolt says quietly, "When he left the organization, they planned to have him executed. I offered myself into Malakai's inner circle as payment for Torin's life. I had no choice, Everett. If I didn't collect Arryn, everything I did would have been for nothing, and Torin's life would have been forfeited."

My heart sinks.

"I left everything behind. Everything I had, I left behind."

Vanessa... everything clicks into place with his words.

I knew they had history and the pain I see in Kolt's eyes is the same pain I felt when I woke to Arryn's letter.

"He gave me my freedom and Torin's life in exchange for Arryn. And it's now my time to fix what I broke."

"I forgive you," Arryn speaks from behind me. "I don't blame you."

I turn to find her standing behind me, her face soft and understanding and behind her, Torin stares at Kolt, pale and devastated.

We never knew. Neither of us knew.

Kolt was free and Torin was safe, and Olivia had just given her life to save Arryn and me.

Malakai just kept taking. He just kept stealing lives and time.

"We'll take Olivia back to Ravenpeak," I sigh, "Until he calls, she can stay there with us."

"I have a hotel to run," She stands and lets out a breath, some color back in her cheeks. "Arryn deserves happiness, Everett. Don't hurt her."

The *or else* was implied.

CHAPTER FORTY-FOUR
arryn

I convinced Olivia to come back with us, at least for a few weeks. The Lauder hotel had management more than capable of running the place while we spent some time together.

But before we all, including Kolten, get on that boat, Oli and I take a walk down to the cemetery.

It was cold this morning, the sky overcast with winds that whipped at our hair and nipped at whatever skin we had on show. I was able to go back to my place and grab some things which Rett took with him while they waited for us to return.

But this was the first time I was getting to say goodbye to my father.

Olivia hadn't properly mourned either, not when she was also trying to find me.

Her hand grips mine tightly but I don't complain at the pinch in my knuckles because of it. She looked ill, exhausted and I was hoping the next two weeks or more would bring her back to life.

And then she was going to marry Malakai. The same man who had a hand in our father's murder. Olivia had explained what Malakai had told her about that night. Kenneth had found out about the hit my father ordered and decided to retaliate using the man in charge of the whole thing. It was never about the hotel itself, never about money or power, it was about vengeance. And I happened to be in the way.

Malakai hadn't expected Rett to show up which had caught him off guard. After we faked my death and the images were sent, Malakai realized where we were and used it to his advantage. He played the long game, waited us out and we showed him our asses.

It was all a game.

And that just made me even angrier. There was no getting one up on this man, this so-called king of the underworld. He was a devil. A king of hell. And my sister just agreed to marry him to save me.

And there was nothing I could do about it.

Absolutely nothing.

The gate squeaks loudly in the otherwise quiet graveyard, the church standing tall and ominous ahead of us. Gravestones line either side of us, some pristine marble, fresh and clean, others aged and worn, cracked, and covered in moss, the names on the stones long since distorted by time.

"We buried him next to mom," Olivia whispers as if speaking any louder may disturb the dead that lay all around us.

"I watched it," I admit, hiding the way my voice cracks around the lump in my throat.

Olivia nods, "I just wanted you there. It's all I could think about. I was so scared Arryn."

I give her hand a squeeze "I know. And I hate myself for not being here."

"It wasn't your fault."

We walk, both silent, our feet crunching over gravel and sopping leaves until we come to a fresh grave. The earth is freshly turned, the gleaming white marble headstone looking so awfully out of place next to the much older one of my mothers.

Fresh flowers have been placed in front of the stone and more flowers are in front of my mother's too, "You?"

"No." Olivia shakes her head.

Behind us a branch snaps and I spin around, still jumpy from the past few weeks. A shadow moves at the side of the church, there and then gone.

"Can you say goodbye now?" Olivia hisses, "Graveyards creep me the fuck out."

Despite the obvious warning that someone was watching us, I laugh and crouch close to my father's headstone, running my fingers over the engraved name.

"Love you, dad," I whisper, "I'm sorry I couldn't say goodbye properly." Kissing my fingers, I place them on his stone before I do the same to my mothers and then we turn around and haul ass out of there.

The walk back towards the docks is done quickly, paranoia that we were being followed making us quicken our step. By the time we are in view of the boat waiting for us, and the men too, both of us are heaving and out of breath, sweat dampening our skin despite the freezing temperatures.

"What's wrong?" Everett asks the moment he sees us.

"There was someone watching us," I huff out, "At the graveyard."

A muscle twitches in his jaw and he looks over my shoulder as if he'd spot whoever was still there. "Get on the boat. We're leaving."

I don't ask questions and accept Torin's hand as he helps me and then Olivia into the boat.

"I get seasick," Olivia grits her teeth.

"So do I," my head snaps up at the voice. Kolten offers a bottle of pills to Olivia, the label worn so I can't see what they are, "They'll help with the nausea."

But when we both just stare at him like he has two heads, he pops the cap and takes a pill himself, "It won't hurt you." He assures.

I leave my sister to take the pills and cross over to Rett who helps Torin get us prepared to move away.

His hand instantly falls to the small of my back and he glances at me, any hardness in his face softening the moment his eyes meet mine.

It makes me melt a little, the way he looks at me.

"It's time to go home," he says to me.

The sentence brings so much damn joy to my heart I feel as if I may float. "Home," I agree.

"To start making all those babies," Everett wiggles his eyebrows.

Laughter bubbles out of me as his arm wraps around my waist and he tugs me in close, his lips crashing down onto mine.

"I love you," He whispers on my mouth, the words tasting like sugar on my tongue.

"I love you too, Everett Avery."

The boat rocks over the sea, the city behind growing smaller and smaller as we sail toward Ravenpeak Bay.

With his hand on mine and a whole life ahead of us, I realize this wasn't the end of our fairytale but the beginning.

EPILOGUE
arryn

Five years later...

The sun beats down brightly, the summer heat almost unbearable. Pulling my hair away from the nape of my neck I step up onto the porch of the cabin for some shade and relief from the sun. We were surrounded by trees; you'd expect some shade but no.

But my little vegetable garden was coming along nicely. Turns out, I like to garden. Boring I know but the mundane tasks like pruning roses and getting pricked by thorns was something never offered to me. Rett says the novelty will wear off, but it's been two years since I started doing it and I haven't lost interest yet.

HURRICANE

Not like the crocheting or candle making I attempted previously, or the several other hobbies before that.

I didn't have time before, but I do now. In between managing the lingerie business which I mostly did online, with the occasional trip back to the factories and warehouses that were few and far between. I had piles of sketchbooks with new designs all being worked on but in between that, I did this.

Rett mostly watched while I did it, he tried to help once or twice but that man was like a bull in a China shop around plants, he trampled my flowers, so he was banned from them.

Speaking of Rett, he was supposed to be home by now.

He'd taken Walker, our three year old son, down into town to spend time with Maya and Torin and their brood but that was hours ago. I glance towards the clock, maybe I was wrong, but the clock shows the right time.

Pulling out my cell, I dial his number.

"Took you long enough little storm," He rasps into my ear, answering on the first ring.

"What happened?" I gasp, picturing horrendous things, "Are you hurt?"

"Why not come and find me, princess?" His husky tone whips awareness through me and my eyes snap to the thick wall of trees in front of me, "Or perhaps you can go for a wander, and I'll find you."

"And what happens if you find me?" I breathe, knowing exactly what will happen.

"Are you bare under that pretty yellow dress, little storm?"

I lift my dress, still on the phone with my husband and shimmy my underwear down my legs before I lift them and dangle the lace off my finger. I knew he could see me, he was in those trees somewhere, hidden and waiting. I wave the underwear like a flag.

"I am now."

"Run little storm," Rett growls down the phone, "I am starving and right now you look good enough to fucking eat."

"Promises," I step down off the porch and into the sun, "I don't mind playing your games since even when I lose, I always win."

He chuckles and I hang up, taking a deep breath before I take off in a run.

We've played this game, many, many times, sometimes it lasts hours, sometimes it takes minutes.

I was needy this time, he always made me needy so perhaps I'll make it easy on him.

He's trained me some in the years that have passed, how to be quiet, how to be stealthy and he often curses how well he taught me since I've escaped him more times than he likes to admit.

I start through the trees, my footing light to save making any noise as I run. I use trees to swing myself around, throwing myself deeper into the woods but I know he's behind me. I feel his presence, gaining space.

I make a jump over a fallen tree and turn, only to run right into a hard, bare chest.

"Hello princess," He grins down at me, his skin gleaming with sweat, his smile mischievous and playful, full of sinful promises.

"Oh no," I feign disappointment, "You caught me."

His deep chuckle starts right before his hands clasp me behind the thighs and he lifts, forcing me to wrap my legs around his waist. He was already hard, pressing against me through the material of his pants.

He finds a clear spot and gets to his knees, guiding me down onto my back, right there in the middle of the forest.

Somewhere close by, I hear the voices of hikers trying to make their way to the peak and my voice gets lodged in my throat.

"Rett," Wide eyes meet his.

"Don't want to get caught, little storm, you better be quiet. I told you I was starving and I'm not waiting."

His hands eagerly shove up my dress, finding me bare and wet for him and as he stated, he eats like a damn man starved. I slap my own hand over my mouth to stop my cries as he works me expertly, licking and sucking the sensitive and tender flesh into his mouth as his fingers penetrate me, thrusting into me as he works me up and up.

The sky and trees swirl above me, the pleasure almost too much and not enough all the same. His fingers work harder and faster, my cries becoming louder and harder to stifle.

And then I detonate against his mouth, spine arching away from the forest floor as the wave rushes through me.

He doesn't wait for me to stop before he shoves out of his pants and slams into me in one hard, sure thrust, filling me and stretching me to fit him.

"So good, princess," He moans, "So fucking good."

"Don't stop," I plead, clawing at his back, nails scoring his skin.

His teeth nip at my skin, the bite of pain only adding to the intense pleasure wracking my entire system.

With every thrust he goes deeper, pushing me closer to the second release.

"Goddamn," Everett rasps, "I can never get enough of you."

My nails sink in, likely drawing blood as he pushes me over that final ledge, my climax shaking my whole body and bringing on his.

He lands at my side, the two of us a sweaty, breathless mess. I could feel him leaking out of me, my thighs still shaking with the effects of what he does to me.

Our whole life now was as perfect as I could have ever wished for.

We are a fairytale.

And it didn't matter how many storms we had to battle to get here, it's that we made it. There was a clear horizon ahead, and forever had only just begun.

RAVENPEAK BAY
RJ WILDE

Lake
HURRICANE

Thank you!

Thank you so much for taking the time to read Like a Hurricane! Everett has been screaming in my head ever since I introduced him back in TRW! The charming Avery brother needed his story and I hope you've enjoyed it as much as I have!

So what's next? Of course, our third and final brother is up next! It's angsty, painful and beautiful all the same. The Ravenpeak Bay Series will continue with Beneath These Dark Skies.

But that's not all. I couldn't introduce Malakai Farrow without giving him and Olivia a story! Playing with Fire is coming summer 2024! It will be a complete standalone to the Ravenpeak Bay series as a dark, arranged marriage standalone romance.

beneath these
DARK SKIES

RAVENPEAK BAY
BOOK III

RIA WILDE

playing with fire

an arranged marriage standalone

RIA WILDE

MORE FROM RIA WILDE

TWISTED CITY DUET

LITTLE BIRD – BOOK 1
TWISTED KING – BOOK 2
TWISTED CITY – THE COMPLETE SET

WRECK & RUIN

WICKED HEART
SAVAGE HEART

STANDALONES

NO SAINT
ALL THE BROKEN PIECES
PRETTY RECKLESS
PLAYING WITH FIRE

RAVENPEAK BAY

THESE ROUGH WATERS
LIKE A HURRICANE
BENEATH THESE DARK SKIES

ABOUT THE AUTHOR!

Ria Wilde is an author of dirty, dark and dangerous romance. A lover of filthy talking anti-heroes and sassy AF queens! She's always had a love of reading and decided to pursue her passion of words in late 2021 and hasn't looked back since! Little Bird and Twisted King, Ria's debut dark romance was the start of something amazing and she now has plans for several new series and spin-offs with some of your favorite characters as the main stars!

She currently resides in the UK with her husband, daughter and 2 dogs. You can often find her daydreaming or procrastinating with her head buried in a book!

STALK ME

www.riawilde

Made in the USA
Middletown, DE
03 October 2024